Where the Birds Don't Sing

A Path to Sobriety,
The Inside Passage

A Romance in Augsburg
[Volume I of III]

Romancing San Francisco
[Volume II of III]

Death on Demand
[Seven Suspenseful Short Stories]

The Mumbler,
Murder by the Second Self

✳

The Mumbler,
The Poetry of a Killer
[Companion]

Death by Desire
[Nine Stores of Suspense]

Where the Birds Don't Sing
[Volume III of III]

The Fruit Cake
[A Comady-Tradgy]

✳

Where the Birds Don't Sing

◆

[How it was, Sketches of Life in 1971-Vietnam]

[Volume III to the Chick Evens Trilogy]

Dennis L. Siluk
[Staff Sergeant US Army 1969–1980]

iUniverse, Inc.

New York Lincoln Shanghai

Where the Birds Don't Sing
[How it was, Sketches of Life in 1971-Vietnam]

iUniverse, Inc.

For information address:
iUniverse, Inc.
2021 Pine Lake Road, Suite 100
Lincoln, NE 68512
www.iuniverse.com

Credit for graphic art [drawing] by the
Dlsiluk, l980, Original with black ink

ISBN: 0-595-28180-X

Printed in the United States of America

*"Those who cannot remember the
past are condemned to repeat it."*

—George Santayana

*If I have learned anything, one thing
Stands out—nothing is for sure, in war;—on the
Other hand, anything is possible.*

—D.L. Siluk

＊

Contents

Vietnam

Introduction xvii

Preface xix

Introductory Chapter:
A Night with Tequila [before Vietnam] 1

CHAPTER 1   Cam Ranh Bay 9

CHAPTER 2   The Bay and Frenchie 17

CHAPTER 3   Raquel Welch 22
          [And three poems]

CHAPTER 4   Who Heard Me. 25

CHAPTER 5   The Bomb. 27

CHAPTER 6   The Last Fight. 30

CHAPTER 7   Rockets at the Ammo Dump. 39

CHAPTER 8   Engagements. 44

CHAPTER 9   The Truck. 50

CHAPTER 10   Free Supplies and the Feud 53

CHAPTER 11   The Scorpion. 58

CHAPTER 12   Vietnam the Country 60

Australia R&R [Sydney]

"New south Wales—Queensland"

CHAPTER 13   Girl from the Farm 65

CHAPTER 14   The Park in Queensland 69

CHAPTER 15   The New Zealand Maids 71

CHAPTER 16   The Bar-Party and Demi 73

CHAPTER 17   The Bill 78

Vietnam

CHAPTER 18   Saigon-Going Home The Cage and the
             Stranger 80
             [Thoughts on the airplane going to Ft. Lewis]

CHAPTER 19   A Steak at Fort Lewis 86
             [24-hours to freedom]

St. Paul

CHAPTER 20   Back Where I Started 89

  • *Ye Little Birds* *90*

Last Words 93

End to the Story 95

About the Author's Books 97

Special Thanks to my Wife
Rosa and Jon McWilliams

Farewell to the Birds

There is a place on this earth
Where the birds don't sing,—
Where the troops march,
Eating dust and rain;—
Always wondering
Where the birds went
As they swiftly move away
When one gets off the plane:—
"Farewell!" they sing, "Farewell!"
"See you
Another day…"

—Dlsiluk, Vietnam 1971

Scroll

"Memory is when you look back
And the answer floats in
To who? What? When? Where?
…
Sometimes slurred and blurred—
This Remembering—
…proceeding again to reconstruct
What happened and how…"

—Carl Sandburg

◊

All sciences natural or not, everything in general to include 'war'—needs a logical system for understanding:—something that was missing in Vietnam, unfortunately.

Chick Evens

Introduction

A confession: In fact it took me four months to write this book, although only 4-minutes to conceive it; and yet, 33-years to get to it, and eight months to live it—

My idea to write came in October 2002, prior to going to Lima, Peru to visit my wife's relatives, and other friends. I felt a need to connect my prior two volumes "*Romancing San Francisco*," and "*A Romance in Augsburg*," together—.

And so, I write of my youthful generation, 32-years past, for this generation of critics now, and for those who simply wish to know.

≡

I am not really all that much for introductions,—they seem to use up a lot of valuable time and space that should really be intertwined into the story and so I will make this brief at best. This is the third part to *The Chick Evens Trilogy*. It started with the book, "*Romancing San Francisco*," where karate and a number of other things were brought into the ongoing saga of Chick Evens. There you met Gosei Yamaguchi, world karate champion, and a host of other people, events, and things happening; sketches of life of the late sixties if you will, or better put, a slice of life. The time period was 1968-69. From there we went to the second book of the trilogy, which is, "*A Romance in Augsburg*," taking place in 1970, where the main character [Chick Evens] gets drafted out of San Francisco, goes back to St. Paul, and into the Army, and to be quite honest, it is just one of a few romance involved in the trilogy but the most profound in the trilogy; "*Romancing San Francisco*." But as I was saying, "*Romancing San Francisco*," its theme in particular, had more to do with Karate per se,—the novel being the catalyst to the trilogy—the stepping stone if you will.

And now for the last part of the trilogy, which takes place in 1971, in Vietnam, and here again, you get war, affairs, some adventure, and a trip to Australia where a few other things take place. All three novels consume 27-months of active time [with 15-months of in-between time; which I call lingering time]; thus, making it a forty-two month saga in total. The sketches are linked together, as are all three

xviii   Where the Birds Don't Sing

novels. It starts from the summer of 1968, and ends in the fall of 1971. Some may find this a bit different, as far as a novel goes, because of the sketches, but it is no different than some of the books or short stories linked together as sketches done in the 1920's throughout the 40's.

> "Americans believe in freedom and the dignity of man. They back that belief with action. The Americans in Vietnam know war at first hand. They see it for what it is. War is fear cloaked in courage. It is excitement overlaying boredom. It is close friendships, with loneliness only a thought away. It is compassion in the midst of destruction. It is dedication winning over weariness and frustration. War is paying a terrible price today for a better tomorrow....
>
> The Major Kelly's—and the Private Smith's and all the others—have given America more than they have taken from her. And they are still giving..."

> General William C. Westmoreland
> [Commander, U.S. Forces in Vietnam]

The Story:
"Where the Birds Don't Sing"
Preface

≈

A Letter to the Editor by Chick Evens, 1972

"It was a decade of change and challenges for the world, America in particular, it was 'The New Generation,' that's what we were calling it I guess, the Age of Aquarius was around the corner. For me it started in 1967 in St. Paul Minnesota when I decided to join it by preparing to leave my nice little city by the Mississippi, and it wouldn't stop for me until December 1971, we might just as well say 1972. In any case, the 60's and early 70's produced an avalanche of changes. As I went from St. Paul, the conservative city of culture, to San Francisco, the radical city of the west, and onto West Germany, for a romance that would stick to me like glue for many years to come, and over to Vietnam, for a war that had many limitations, some expectations, and too many variables. In this short time of 42-months, between the Summer of 1968 and the fall of 1971, the long hair, mod dress [hippies], drugs, sexual freedoms, anti-establishment ideas where much more plentiful, one might say, than ten years prior to this. The so called, 'New Generation,' had a romantic fever within its veins. Actually, between 1959 and 1965, such things would have been unbelievable. But it is how it was, and I was in the heart of it.

Chick Evens

A Night with Tequila

[Post, San Francisco:—1969]

I was in-between going into the Army, which would bring me to Augsburg, Germany, and then on to Vietnam, and leaving San Francisco, where I had lived for a year, and practiced karate with the famous Gosei Yamaguchi, and worked for the famous cloth designing company, Lilli Ann. Thus, leaving San Francisco, I went down to Southern California to meet with my brother, he and I then ventured down to Mexico for a day where I bought a bottle of tequila, with the worm in it. This would prove to be an adventure in itself, with an unforgettable night, linger in the future; notwithstanding, I will leave out the trouble that took place in Mexico, and be thankful we got out in one piece, and with my bottle of Tequila: and leave it at that, but let me add, the beer was heavy, and we almost got in a fight with several Mexican Soma-type looking wrestlers. In any event, we did make it out alive, as you are reading this, and therefore I must have.

And then on to [back to that is] St. Paul, Minnesota our home city and state;—my brother, myself, his wife and two-kids went by car, and yes I carried my bottle of Tequila, all the way. I had never drunk the stuff before, and figured I'd save it for a special occasion, hoping it would come soon. Plus, it would be a new experience for me when I did drink it, that is to say, showing everyone that damn famous worm, everyone talks about. When you moved the bottle of Tequila about—you could actually see the worm floating every which way.

We spent a day in Salt Lake City, Utah, as we had found a cheap, small motel close to the inner city; my brother's wife got chased back to the motel for being out past 10:00 PM without her husband, as she was trying to buy some groceries.

I think we had a good laugh on that, that evening.

I didn't see much of the city, although I did look for a few bars, I guess everything was either underground, or they had some secret black market where they hid the booze, but there was no chance for a nice cold beer, I figured that out quick. In any case, the night came quick, and we all slept well; the morning came quick also.

We took turns—that is, my brother and I took turns driving his car over the long dusty roads, but the weather was pleasing, a bit warm yet it made driving comfortable.

When we arrived in St. Paul, it was but a few weeks before my brother decided to head on up to North Dakota, Grand Forks, to help put in a cement platform, for a garage in, helping out his father-in-law. I told him I'd go along and help if he didn't mind, and it all seemed quite productive, for the most part. And when the day arrived to leave'—yes again, I carried my bottle of Tequila all the way to the Dakota's with me: almost as if it was a gift from the god's.

✳

As we arrived in Grand Forks, we all stayed at my brother's father-in-law's house, the very house we were to do the construction work at, in the back yard. The hot weather was starting to leave the Midwest, and the cooler air was coming down from Canada, as September crept in slowly. It was a good time to work the construction part, that is, without sweating to death. The Midwest was extremes, hot in the summer and cold in the winter. In fall, it was perfect, especially for construction.

As I got to meet the rest of my sister-in-law's family, I think I must have been saving this bottle of Tequila for this occasion, for I had a sense it was not going to make it back home. I had hid the bottle in my brother's car, and drank beer the first night I was there with the rest of the relatives. His wife had several bothers and we all sat around getting drunk,—talking about how we were going to go about building the wooden frame of the foundation, to pour the cement for the garage: that is, the ground work was already done, leveled and the wooden frame needed to be made, this could be done quickly in the morning with long two-by-four boards, thereafter, we'd do the cement work, and then we'd stay an extra day and have a get together, kind of celebration. It all sounded grand.

During this time I had met Paula, a friend of the family. I was twenty years old, and she was seventeen, we both seemed somewhat attracted to one another—time would tell.

✳

As we worked all day the following day on the cement, digging a foundation, putting up sides-boards to pour the cement, and measuring, along with putting in other sources of support like, stones etc., we finally did pour the cement, and it turned out better than what I had hoped for. We really did not need professionals, only a good thought out plan, effort, and a gathering of the willing.

Now it was party time. Paula told me to skip the get together with the family at my brother's wife's house, for the time being, and head on to her friend's house, and join their party this evening, and we'd come back to join the family workers later, for they also would be having a party. It all sounded reasonable to me.

As we got to the party [7:00 PM] Paula introduced me to several of her young friends, and I pulled out from underneath my jacket the bottle of Tequila I had purchased in Mexico, the one with the worm in it.

Paula said,

"What is that thing in the bottle?" As she was reading the label that said 'Tequila,' on it, she added, "I heard of this stuff, it's pretty strong, isn't it?"

[A rhetorical question at best] "It's a genuine worm alright," I clarified, adding, "…that is what indicates it's the original Mexican thing." I really didn't know what I was talking about—for the most part—but whatever the 'thing [worm], meant,' none the less, made for good conversation.

As we sat on the sofa in the living room of her friend's house I checked Paula out, I liked her, she looked a little French-Canadian, that is to say, she had a natural tan to her skin, almost olive. She had short black hair, a shapely body, to include a pear like base [or underneath—about 5' 3" inches tall, stunning looks, a real beauty.

We both had a few of the beers the folks at the party offered, and then I opened up the Tequila.

She asked me [pleadingly-with a touch of humor] "Should I try to drink the worm when it surfaces out of the bottle or see if it comes out of the bottle while I pour it into my glass, and then drink it?"

"Forget the glass, take a swig right out of the spout, and if you get the worm, swallow it. That's the best way to do it. Let's see who gets to it first." We both smiled at one another, and down the 'hatch' we drank our first, longgggg-shot. I drank about three shots at once,—along with taking some salt at the same time putting it on my hand and licking it; someone had told me to do it, it was actually a little more agreeable with the salt, the Tequila that is. And then Paula did the same. No one got the worm; we again looked at one another and laughed.

"Ham m," we both hummed at each other.

"Let's try again," I said contentedly...

As the night went on, a few of the folks from my brother's wife's family, along with my brother came over to the party to check on Paula and me. They saw we were drinking away like two silly kids. I was now 21-years old, I could legally drink, but Paula wasn't,—I think they were more worried about Paula, being 17, and I suppose I may have looked a little dangerous to my sister-in-law, being with her younger sister.

They sat by us and had a few drinks of the Tequila, and then feeling all was well and under control left us to ourselves. They were only up the block about four houses in any case, meaning, if they needed to run to her rescue, they could. I think they were afraid I'd steal her away and run to Minnesota with her,—or her with me. We were just having a good ol'-time, no more, no less.

At 11:00 PM, Paula asked if we should call it a night, we were both getting pretty drunk.

"No, no," I said, "Let's finish the whole bottle and whoever ends up with the worm is the winner." [Although the winner only got the worm.]

"Ok, Ok," she atheistically said, at first glance.

1:00 PM

[Halfheartedly I told Paula.] "It looks like my turn to drink." Yet, I could hardly find the bottle, let alone see the worm. At great length I put my hand out to grab the bottle:

"Ok, here it is," I took a big drink, "...the worm is still in there Chick," Paula commented. I looked I couldn't see it, "I must of drank it," I replied, no answer.

Morning

Paula [who has risen] "Who got the worm?" she asked, no answer. She moved about, trying to stretch, laying on the floor next to me, where she had passed out, and I on the sofa had passed out right along with her [a pause].

"I think I got it," I grabbed the bottle on the floor with the Tequila label on it, it was empty, and the worm was gone.

"I think I ate it, or swallowed it, and then I must have passed out," I explained to her [a little stiffly].

"No," she replied, "I think you tried to get the worm out, and couldn't, and there was a little substance left, and I had the next try, and got it out." We looked at each other [wearily] struggling to put on a smile and started laughing. Whoever got the worm we would never know for sure? But one of us did.

"I think Paula," I commented, "…we both ate the worm, I got half and you got half. If I recall right, I got the worm out safe and sound, and poured the rest of the Tequila in a glass, and cut the worm in half, and we both had the last drink together each getting half the worm."

"Really," she said, [after listening for a moment].

"Absolutely," I wasn't sure of anything, but I dreamt it or for some reason it came out naturally. Who knows after you drink a fifth of Tequila what happened to the worm, maybe it walked away. Whatever the case, Paula was a little more agreeable with that ending to the worm.

Vietnam

1971

◊

I doubt in any war you'll find the birds singing:—
I never did hear them in Vietnam, nor did I hear the
Sounds of Americans hooraying their heroes as they
Came home;—there was really nothing for a Soldier
Except another Soldier in those far off days.

◊

1

Cam Ranh Bay

[Vietnam-1971]

In a war zone,—a combat zone that is, or for that matter, in a support unit that is in a war zone, there are very few flags flopping out in the wind, or for that matter, finding soldiers standing erect with dressed greens, gloriously waiting for combat around the bend [like in the movies], sorry, just squads of the military marching, trampling through the rain and mud, dodging bullets, rockets.

The soldiers in Vietnam, for the most part young men, were a little frazzled in the nerves trying to figure out where they fit in, in the scheme of all things that is. Having said that, what was the objective [that is what we all asked ourselves sooner or later]:—to win, stabilize, or contain? Nothing was clear except one thing, or so I found out soon after I arrived in Vietnam, it was not to be won, that is the war, that is, won in the sense of a straight out victory.

Whatever was on the political minds of the decision makers in Washington D.C., the soldiers didn't know, but it was not to win the war. For we all knew it was or could have been a simple task. But then we did not want to incite Russia, did we, that was our way of avoiding a nuclear confrontation I suppose; likewise, in Korea, we did not want to incite China, and face a nuclear stand off in that area, that is to say, we'd have had to use those big bombs to stop the horde of oncoming enemy soldiers. Or at least that was the way our decision makers were thinking, or so I think.

Back to Vietnam, again, I do not think it would have been a hard war to win [had we not put limitations on ourselves, and overlooked targets for the sake of getting other nations mad at us], but then you had your negative forces working against you/or us, such as Jane Fonda's [see also Last Words] in addition to the indecisive political minds in Washington D.C., and throughout the states...that made it harder. [As in many wars, you get your wild radicals, even in the Persian Gulf II War, such as Sean Penn, and a few like him.] All wanting to arouse our emotions to go see their movies, and side with them on a protest march, but when you protest against them, they get emotional unstable, they don't like it [like President George W. Bush, said, "…it's a two way street…"]. And in most cases the protesters such as they are, have never seen a day of combat, but there is not lack of wisdom with them.

My way of protesting would be when I got home out of Vietnam, I would not go see their movies, although I did see one, and purchased another, but it was very hard for me to watch them. I guess big movie stars have an edge they can get on stage and can give their opinion to millions of people in a matter of minutes, someone like me, well, my only way is, or was, saying it by not supporting them in whatever way possible. Some people feel this way is not the right way to respond, but it's the only way I know, and a non-violent way I knew, and it's a good old American style way of protesting, I know.

And from what I've seen of such times and events, most people couldn't tell the difference between being assertive, which I think is healthy in protesting one's view in war or peace, and aggressiveness, which I think is hypocritical at best. But that's the way it always is. You go on a peace march, and create a war. To me a peace march should be peaceful and so on and so on, but we see the creation of hysteria; exactly what are they protesting, should it not be their own behavior? But that was the way I was thinking at the time.

Life in general in Vietnam [in a support group environment as I was in] had its regular duties as back home, or in Germany, you were cleaning rifles, washing socks, grabbing the warm rain and using it for a shower. The married men were trying not to feel the pain of missing wives; I got a *Dear John Letter,* saying, my gal from Augsburg, Germany, was no longer going to write me:—as I expected, but I did my grieving on leave in St. Paul, Minnesota, a tear, a river destroyed, or was it two rivers, whatever, I can't remember anymore, it was too long ago. In war it is best you leave the love letters behind.

But it was over [the relationship in Augsburg], and I was glad, I didn't want to end up doing like the other guys,—that is, you hurry up and wait for the mail bag to arrive hoping you get a letter or two, day after day you give power and control of your life to that person to decide what and when to write you,—this all plugs up your mind. You think '…do I go to war today, die and go to hell, or do you think I'll make it home.' This begs the question, who wants to live, for surely Charlie, the enemy does, and as I always said, I do, and I said I'd go home all together, or not at all, and if Charlie got in my way, we'd both go to hell together. But the married men always wanted to go home; were thinking about home. And you knew what was on their mind most of the time: especially if they were, or had been married a short time, they always seemed preoccupied. In a combat zone this can be dangerous.

I didn't want dark foot steps to awaken me in my sleep, while in Vietnam, so with one eye open I slept all the time while in Vietnam, and if a shadow crossed my path, he would die, or wish he had.

On other occasions, some of my comrades would say,

"Why do you keep your rifle always locked and loaded…?" meaning ready to shoot, "…even when you know Charlie is up in the hills, two miles away, somewhat harmless, if only he stays there." My response was always,

"I liked it loaded,—it makes me feel good, like I'm in control, the way I want it to be." It would worry some of my friends, that being, afraid I'd shoot them by accident. And I suppose anything was possible.

✳

Vietnam was many things to me, one might say, that being a pocket full of experiences, somewhat like, but not quite like, Augsburg, Germany, where I ended up in a romance, yup, that was where I was stationed prior to coming to Vietnam. And San Francisco was also quite a learning experience, which was where I was living for a year prior to going into the Army, and being sent to Augsburg. Somehow they all seem to connect because they all blended into one another, ending up here in Vietnam.

Some of my new experiences would entail heroin usage, and finding me dancing on top of a vacant supply-hut in the middle of the jungle, where I and four other soldiers were dismantling the metal supply hut. Again, here we were dancing on the top of the roof, listening to music some of Bob Dylan, I think, and the Turtles, etc., as if there was no war. I still kept my M16 locked and loaded though;—but god forbid should the enemy come; I'd had left it down on the ground by some other garments I put. I'd have had to jump off the roof to get to my weapon, by that time we'd all be dead.

After several hours of our rope-a-dope adventure, we had the place all dismantled, so Charlie could not use it and we then went back to base camp. That was my first usage of the white gold, heroin. Three dollars a capsule and you could smoke it, rub it in your veins, or for that matter, inject it; however you liked it. It was so good I told myself, this was not going to happen again. I would surely end up a dope freak, and this was not the place for it.

As the sun was disappearing that day, we had made it back to our hutches in time for dinner. We had white rice with eggs, hamburger and green peppers all mixed and fried together, it was great.

✻

In the ammo dump, as we called it [ammo supply area], where I'd work now and then, I swatted flies all day it seemed in the little wooden shack we used for an office. And to be quite frank, that in itself is a tiring job, especially if there is no wind cross-venting the place. And just try not swatting them, they eat you alive, that is, they land on everything, everywhere, all day long.

Outside of the hut, was the copper sun descending on top of you as if you could touch the sphere itself; you could cook an egg out on a rock, one of the soldiers tried it, it works. Often times when things got slow, and they often did, you'd be day-dreaming on the porch of the hut, or walking around looking for a stick to wipe your ass with, for there was no toilet paper.

The ones with wives, or lovers back home, were lovesick half time, truly lost in the heat and rains of Vietnam; again I say this because it was cause for alarm at times. I often thought of the Israel Army, to my understanding if a person had gotten married, they would not allow him into the service for a year or so. That made good sense, he had his sex, got his house in order for the most part; and was focused.

Nights seemed star-less, no birds singing at all, matter of fact, there were no birds. Not in the jungle, or out in the ammo dump, only dry-heat, lizards and not too far away the South China Sea coast. No birds, no birds, no sir, never-ever heard them, no birds at all—and if there were I had never seen them. [As I write this I can hear them now outside my windows, chirping, and singing. What a lovely sound!]

✻

It seemed to me I'd make it through Vietnam alive, I guess I never thought I wouldn't as long as I was breathing and not bleeding. One of my friends got out the hard way, he screwed so many women so he got all these different kinds of venereal disease, some I never heard of, and had to get sent to Japan for treatment. His spine was bent over backwards, like the Hunchback of Notre Dame.

We'd talk at night, and he told me point blank, "Chick, I fuck sometimes three times a day."

I said, "You got to stop, look what it's doing to you," that was a month before he got this disease the 5th time, or was it the 7th? In any case, this time he had a hard time looking up at me, he was so bent over from spine problems, and talking was too painful I could tell, and the next day he was gone. What a way to go, no combat, just bad company. I guess we all chose our sins, and our own way of dealing with them and the unknown, along with boredom and the funny rules they had over here: and most of the ways we dealt with such issues like that were by disassociation [blocking your mind to/or from reality], be it by sex, dope, gambling, fighting, or booze, like I chose often, or whatever was available. I guess war is to be war, not sitting around waiting for the pizza man. That is to say, we should be fighting or training, not doing what we were doing.

♀

And so here I am in Vietnam, the year is 1971, halfway around the world, with no poets, no rich people, no lawyers, but one of the guys named Presley, was a relative of Elvis' [or so he said]. Anyways, the rich and famous were not present, isn't it always that way? It simply told you, who is and who isn't dispensable to the government. No disrespect intended, for I do not mind being here, I have no better place to be, no one waiting for me at home, no girl that is. So to me it is simply a trip in the jungle, along the sea coast.

My Hutch

It was the winter of 1971 I lived in a hutch at an Army Base in Cam Ranh Bay, Vietnam, looking up and across the dry white sand, and hard-dirt that compressed against the hills surrounding our camp, there was a radar station, right above us. Down by the shore, the coast of the South China Sea, there were a few shrines, temples hidden in the jungle, and a road that lead out to three ammo dumps, Alpha, Charlie and Delta [Alpha being the Air Force dump]. The sand was dry and white, actually perfect for a beach for swimming, and to paraphrase a rumor, there had been talk about this area being turned into a resort type area after the war, it could very well make a good area for a resort, with some financial planning and capitol, it could be perfect, it was actually in the air, or should I say, under consideration, with some American businessmen. I couldn't picture it as a resort to be realistic, but who knows, dumber things have happened I told myself. War does not always allow you to see two pictures at once, the present and the potential. But it could be reconstructed to be a resort.

I belonged to the 611th Ordnance Company, there were 167-troops to include myself; with two rolls of hutches in our camp site, [four men to a hut]; a mess hall across from the hutches, of which, in-between was a metal floor extending itself from the hutches to the mess hall with holes in it, which covered the court-yard. A safety measure for all the little and big creatures that wanted to visit us, like snakes, lizards and scorpions, and who knows what else.

We also had an orderly room [main office] in front of our military compound [or camp site/complex], a shower room way in the back of the complex, where the outside toilets were, to the left of it, somewhat isolated though;—not bad for a combated zone compound. And right next to our company, was a Military Police Company [MP's], and their set up was similar to ours. Outside of our compound area was a dusty-dirt road made of compressed hard, very hard dirt on dirt,—well, let me add to that, with some rocks covering the surface also.

✱

Winter in Vietnam was not like winter in St. Paul, Minnesota where I was from. Here in Vietnam, it was hot, hot, muggy and hotter, and at times the humidity was like taking a shower in your hot sweat. There were more lizards than dogs, some as long as six feet. More scorpions than rats, and more jumbo, bull-mosquito's than wasps, yet there were cats, I think we were equal to them in that category in Minnesota vs. Vietnam, or Cam Ranh Bay in particular. Yes, this was a cat lover's haven one might say. But these monster long legged bull-mos-quito's and giant cock-roaches, always flying a foot over your head was enough to keep your mind occupied when you had nothing else to think of, and you found yourself walking about at night with a crown of them over your head;—a giant cockroach falling on your face at night waking you up, and sometimes they would bite you. And if you think they don't bite, you are wrong.

And when I got comfortable in my hutch, I had to spend twenty-minutes out of thirty, killing flies, I know I keep coming back to these fly-issues, but they were everywhere, even in my dreams, yes, instead of sheep jumping over the fence, I had flies I was swatting. But why complain I told myself, I didn't have to comb my hair, shine my boots, or for that matter, dress to impress the brass [officers], not like in Germany. I suppose everything has its bad and good elements to it.

◊

When I had first arrived in Vietnam, it was a shallow evening, the air was thin,—as if you couldn't breath, gently we [the two hundred plus soldiers with me from the jet] were moved onto a metal platform [something like our camp had here], again, I suppose, so the scorpions and the other creatures didn't get to you before Charlie [the enemy] did. We were moved as I said, from the airplane to the platform, and the plane was then pulled away quickly so the enemy could not zero in on it and destroy it. Thereafter, we took busses to this processing center on Cam Ranh Bay. And there in the middle of the night, we waited and waited and waited.

We were like a stream of soldier-ants as long and winding as a football field. And although there were 205,000 soldiers in Vietnam upon my arrival, or so I heard, that was not as many as were here a year prior,—in review, they were withdrawing them slowly, where at one point there were 500,000-plus.

In any event, more were coming and going twice a day from this location, to my understanding.

We didn't know what to expect those first hours, and nothing was happening, just like the old saying goes, 'Hurry up...wait.' The Army is good for that. I only had eight months to go before my tour of duty was up, and I'd get out of the Army, yet I heard they were extending some soldiers an additional six to nine months;—to be quite frank, I met a few that did get extended within a few weeks of their so called leaving Vietnam date. In any case, I felt I could do it standing on my head [the eight months that is] yet, this heat was not doing me much good, and I felt at that time if anything got to me, it would be that.

Being from Minnesota, I was more used to the cold than the heat. Matter of fact, I had spent ten months in Augsburg, Germany just before coming here, and it was a bit nippy, but not bad weather. It seems I adjusted to that easier than I have here—or maybe it was simply familiar back in Germany, and I was fussy with this damn heat.

In Minnesota we actually had extreme hot summers so again maybe my complaining is unfounded, and extreme cold winters. And so I told myself I'd adjust [and so I did]. Likewise, I did appreciate getting away from the snow and cold of both Germany and Minnesota, for the most part.

"Is this it," commented the soldier next to me [while I was waiting with the other 200-soldiers who had first arrived with me in Vietnam].

[I gave him a nod to assure him I was in dismay, or not sure of anything myself] I didn't know him.

Another guy to my far south [about 100-feet] found a pop machine and purchased two cold Coke's, drank them down faster than you can count to ten, and must have shocked his system because of the extreme heat, and dropped over as if he was dead,—but he simply just passed out from the change of body temperature.

[It was February, 1971.] I took off my khaki shirt that day, wiped the dirt from my eyes, and lay back against the wall. Something told me it was going to be an all night and possible all day tomorrow thing, that is, processing me into the country along with the over 200-soldiers with me [and it was].

2

The Bay and Frenchie

[The Village]

Often in the morning as I'd get up, ready to start my duties, I'd see the ARRVIN-Army running by, they were the South Koreans; very disciplined, and seemingly rouged. They'd be running in full dress camouflage uniforms, with heavy boots on, running through the soft white sand the bay area was made out of. Even at night, in the dark they'd run until they couldn't anymore, sometimes right past our company area, as if they never got tired.

On a similar note, on Cam Ranh Bay, there were enough roads built up to run the jeeps here and there, and we had some ¼ [quarter] ton trucks to bring out boxes of ammunition for practice shooting, and we used five-ton trucks for hauling soldiers around: and longer cargo trucks when we had to load or unload ammunition,—supplying units within the area.

In both instances, the trucks were also used to carry troops out to the ammo-dumps, several miles from our base camp.

Over surrounding mountain sides were infested with Viet Cong [the enemy], they had dug in and circled the peninsula of Cam Ranh Bay. It was just a matter of when, and possible if, they were going to come down from up high and attack; and if not attack, covertly steal what they needed for their troops from our ammo dumps; I had often thought the only reason they had not come down to attack was because they could have the village people, who worked for us in the area and convoys, steal what they needed.

They were dug in pretty well [as I had previously mentioned], into holes in the ground, tunnels, like ground hogs:—in small groups they'd be seen by some of our surveillance teams.

Often a number of the Viet Cong [VC] would go down to the local village; about two miles from my base camp and sneak into the village at night and kind of takeover. It seemed to me the Americans had control of the village during the day and the VC at night. I guess to them it seemed 'just' a quite and nice workable situation; both the ammo dumps and the village being near by. Plus, there was electricity in the village, although shut off at 10:00 PM, and turned back on at 10:00 AM the following morning. In comparison to the tunnel they lived in, this was heaven I would guess.

The South Vietnamese, who were on our side, would guard the village fortress-walls night and day from four towers in each corner of the village, looking over the enclosed city, again with its fenced-in walls; I had stayed a number of times overnight there,—yet, none the less, the Viet Cong, I witnessed each time, and through out my nightly stays, continued to roam the streets, were let in willingly by the tower guards [supposedly the guards were on the United States side]. But I didn't want to get into the politics of this, everyone was trying to stay alive, and if appeasing them kept the peace in the village, people looked the other way.

Whatever I couldn't find on base, or at the local PX, I could find on the black market in the village. It was as if they had their own tunnel to the commissary.

Once in the village [and it was off limits for GI's to be in there] you had to get out of the village early in the morning and make sure the tower guards saw you when you left. If you tried at night, they'd shoot you, not knowing who you were [not a very good system]. And so at 6:00 AM, I jumped the fence, while the guards were watching me [and for the most part the VC were also doing the same thing], and I ran back to base camp [like the VC did] some two miles away. When I got into my hutch, I'd pretend I was just getting up, and rushed to make formation in time. Most of the GI's were scared to stay overnight in the main village, or better put, the big village, they'd rather have their girlfriend sneak into their hut at night, and leave in the morning before dawn [the other way around].

One time in the main village, I was quite hungry and a woman I had known had me sit with her and her friends and family to have soup. She said it was pork in the soup, knowing GI's didn't take to eating dog meat; in any event, we all knew [that is to say, the GI's] there were no pigs around in Vietnam—or at least I had never seen any in the bay area, so what else could it be [?] And for the most part, rumor was fact, for I had a friend this happened too, that is, they'd [the Vietnamese] sell the GI's dogs, and come back the next day and sneak them back home. Not sure exactly how it went, but I would guess, they had some kind of system. Thereafter, cook them up and have dinner. Actually they tasted a bit like pork.

At night you could go down to the village at 7:00 PM and pick out a woman who would be standing behind a fence, and take her wherever you wanted to for a price; but when you brought her back, the women needed to walk back through that gate with money, or the *Cowboys* [Young Vietnamese hit gangs] would harass or even beat the girls should she say the GI never gave her a dime. So even if you did not get sex with the female, you still needed to protect her by giving her something to appease the gangs.

I had done this a few times going out to the beach area and grabbing a few kisses from one of the gals behind the fences. But I really didn't have, or for that matter, want to give all the money they wanted for their services. Some GI's gave them two-third's of their check so they would not go out with other GI's;—what they got was a piece of ass [sex] waiting for them nightly. But when they'd go on leave, the girls would screw everyone in the camp for a few extra bucks anyway. Some of the foolish GI's paid them to be faithful while home on leave even, and to my knowledge there were very few that were faithful. I should say, according to my observations. One Vietnamese woman, in particular, even asked me not to let on about her even being in the camp; not to even mention what she was doing for she knew I knew. I suppose it's much like an addiction, sex that is, especially when you make good money, and you enjoy it, and it has been part of your life and occupation for awhile;—much like dope, alcohol, and gambling.

We—the soldiers at 611th Ordnance Company, were [it was winter] tolerant of this, and for the most part, left well enough alone. One reason being, no one wanted to get anyone in trouble, not even the whores, and the other reason being, everyone was fucking them anyways, and so everyone would have to tell on everyone else, so it was best left alone [sad but true, no one was innocent]. And if the soldiers going home were that stupid to give their money away so freely, so be it,—I often would shake my head at them, when they'd tell me such foolishness, and walk away as if to say, be dumb. I figured any man worth his salt, or put another way, anyone dumb enough to do it, deserved to be taken.

Thoughts

[It reminded me of Augsburg, Germany, where a friend of mine, a corporal, was never involved with a girl, until he took a leave one day—after being in Europe going on four years, and met this girl back home in one of the southern states, I can't remember which one, Kentucky I think. Anyhow, I kind of looked up to him [that is, for awhile, until this happened], he saved a hell of a lot of money, and was level headed, until one day when he came back from leave,
    he said,
    "Chick, I met this wonderful girl and I'm going to ask her to marry me."
Yes, just like that.
    Well, I kind of looked surprised. Inasmuch as I respected him, I still had to ask [he looked at me a little guarded when I did ask]:

"Why, you've must have known her from before," for some odd reason it never occurred to me he didn't know her, I was thinking this was old stuff, and he commented,

[Timidly.] "Oh, no, I just met her," then he pulled out a picture of her for me to see. She was a doll, but I told myself, here it comes, the train, he's going to get hit by a train; too close too soon.

"Not that that made any difference." [His voice sounded a little hurt].

"What do you think?" He asked me, carelessly. Well, on one hand I was happy for him; on the other he was being taken. And to me, I felt he could wait, but try and tell someone to wait when they got marriage on their mind, it is better trying or easier, to sober up a drunk. In any case, he couldn't, and wouldn't wait [I just shook my shoulders dumbfounded].

He sold his stereo, and a few other items to accrue some more money, plus, he took all his money in the bank he was saving and went home and married her, then came back to finish his tour of duty a month later.

During the mean time she wrote him a letter saying it was over [that is, with in the following 45-days after he came back to the unit], and he was just blown apart, started drinking, and went crazy. Well, believe it or not, he had to borrow money to go back to the states again, and he tried to patch things up, but putting it back together was not part of her agenda,—when he came back to base in two weeks, he was broke again, crying, and it was over, I mean really over this time.

※

Women can sure damage a good man, or a stupid man, that is, make a stupid man more stupid. I often thought about the sexual gold mind woman have, some know and some do not know they have this;—and some know and will not use it, the sexual gold mind that is,—if you follow me, and if you don't in simple terms, I refer to the poem "The Spider and the Fly," [where the spider tries to coheres the fly to come to her, and no harm will become her, and when the fly does, that is it for the fly, and the spider gets her dinner] they have a sexual weapon they can use to draw us like a magnet, and it's powerful. And so I didn't care to jump on any one thing, girl that is. That's right. No jumping. I took my time, looked at the consequences and tried not to get too emotionally involved while in Vietnam, and avoided all ongoing affairs with women.

One might say I kind of stuck to my own in this area, having a girl called "Frenchie"; she'd sleep with me when she was done with most of the other guys. That is to say, she'd come in my hut in the middle of the night, after making her rounds with the GI's in the company area, push me over in my bunk to the opposite side of the bed and fall to sleep along side of me. If I wasn't tired, and we were both awake, she'd say [with her luring voice],

"Three dollars for you...I give you credit, I feel safe with you, you're my friend." [And she was a friend.] She just liked to screw, and screw and screw, for she could have slept there without offering anything, she knew me well and knew I'd not bother her. She had big breasts, for a small Vietnamese girl, and she'd push them next to me, and get me hard until I couldn't sleep. She must have stayed with me a dozen times during my eight months in Vietnam, until one day the First Sergeant woke me up, and told me to get rid of Frenchie once and for all.

She was a lovely young lady, and those big lovely breasts, and still somewhat firm, unheard of for a Vietnamese girl. She looked more French than Vietnamese, and was taller than most of the girls, about 5'4". She had a very smooth body, and slim waist. Her breasts were very full and healthy looking. She had dark black hair, and dark mystic eyes;—very feminine, and uninhibited. She told me some nights she made $500 dollars, which was a great amount of money for anyone, GI or Vietnamese. She would have had to sleep with thirty guys at least to make that sum. But then some GI's were more willing to pay higher prices for extra things done. She stashed her money under my pillow, or mattress, depending if I was half asleep or not. I'd never touch it; it was always where she put it when she came to get it. Sometimes she'd come back later and get it that evening, that is, she'd drop it off at midnight and pick it up at 4:00 AM in the morning, giving me a good night kiss, and farewell, she was gone, as quick as she came. Sometimes I never knew it was there and she'd come back two days later saying to me, "I left a little bundle under your mattress," and there'd be $300 or $400 hundred dollars. I don't think she wanted to share with the cowboys sometimes. They wanted 20 to 30 percent of what they brought in, and sometimes they would search them completely, having them strip naked in front of them to make sure they were not being cheated. [The cowboys being a group of youth-gang running loose in the village, who made the girls pay for protection; that is protection from other gangs and them.]

3

Raquel Welch

Say what you will, but in my Company area, Raquel Welch was the pin up girl on my wall [black and white], I got a poster from her, signed, but I think it was printed on by machine. No one else in the company had what I called a poster. Calendars yes, but not an original poster, and of Raquel, surely not one from her, so that made me a kind of hot shot [but there is more to this].

Most of my friends in Vietnam believed she [Raquel Welch, whose poster I had put it up on a back-board of the bunk at the head of my bed] was my girlfriend, until I told them, three-weeks after I had gotten it and set it in my room, that I had gotten the poster by request via mailing for it. When I told the guys this, I also told them I was just kidding, that she was not my girlfriend after all—woops, that didn't go over so well, but to make up for it I told them that when I left Vietnam, someone would get it in the company area.

But during the time when they thought she was my girlfriend, the truth of the matter was, they'd come into my hutch, the GI's that is, check out the picture when I was gone, and go tell their friends [sometimes I would ask my hutch buddies '…who was in looking at the picture?' and they'd shoot a few names off to me]. And so, I became quite popular. But again, when I told them the truth, they felt a little dumb, and gave me some dirty looks, but life went on in the hot monsoons, none the less, and they still liked the pin up.

I kept her picture on the back of the board by my bed to the day I left. I had a few takers when I left Vietnam for it, as I had told them I was going to give it away, and I couldn't think of a reason not to give it to them, they'd most likely play the same prank on the new GI's coming into the company as I did. None the less, I did end up giving it to my friend in the mess hall. [I kind of wish I had kept it now that I think about it, a good memory for those long dark lifeless nights, so long ago.] But Raquel thanks for the 6-months of watching over me.

Poetry

[A moment in the present]

One might say my first love was always, or for the most part it seemed to be, either poetry or playing the guitar. One might even add to that by saying, they both went hand-in-hand, poetry in motion that is. In those long lonely far-off nights in Vietnam, between being drunk, guard duty, my regular job, screwing, going to the medic's because I was screwing and got something I'm not proud of, I would sit back and write my poetry, or play my guitar [yes I even found a guitar over there]. Three of my several poems were found recently in one of my old Army Greens I had left in the closet, with the mothballs [in 1980, I would publish my first book of poetry, but I did not add these three poems into them, here they are now]:

[I was sitting back in my bunk, playing the guitar low, looking at my poster of Raquel, and started writing out of the blue…thinking of Minnesota I think "One Autumn Evening, Long, Long Ago,—1971]

<u>I</u>

<u>One Autumn Evening, Long, Long Ago</u>

It burns, burns, burns—with the Flickering of flames and forms:—the warmth it brings to body and soul, and to the fireplace that is no more—.

The sounds—sounds of crackling,—the crackling of the wooden-logs—: say, something was, that once had life, but that something is no more.

And so the shades of Dark Ash—, appear,—replacing the flames and forms—that once were there before—now to be buried, in the bowels of the earth, deep by a tomb, with endless sleep—and that too will change once more…

And so, two fires that once lived, side-by-side—burned, burned, burned alive—! Can no more consume,—as once, as once it did—one autumn evening, long, long ago.

[This next poem "Farting in the Wind', was written while on guard duty 'I hate to say', while at the ammo dump, the only thing in front of me was a dirt road, and I was in my little 4 x 4 guard shack with a big fat riffle that shot two rounds of grenade type missiles; it was a hot and lonely afternoon]

II

Farting in the Wind

You ever fart in the wind—a draft? [Pause, thinking] Farting in the wind is a sin—[did you know that?] Why? Because it is what demons do—; why? How else can they get your attention?

[This poem "Slang in the Rain" was written while on my way to Australia for R&R, from Saigon, on the plane.]

III

Slang in the Rain

Slang is my Rose of beauty, the beauty that makes my stomach ache, my bowels ache, and my mouth dry, my vice stutter—if I remember right.

It is called love to some—but to me, to me it is called, 'Slang in the Rain.' It makes my nights long [when you want to think of some girl you left behind, that now would not give you a ounce of time]. But this rain makes my blood hot, my heart throb, flutter, beat fast. I call it 'Slang in the Rain'—For it is like no other.

It really is like 'Pain in the Ass,' almost like grief…. [Thank god I'm here in Vietnam alone.]

4

Who Heard Me

The second day in Vietnam often times came back to my memory throughout my stay in this hot-hell-hole, when I had time to sit and think after duty hours in my company area. I'd sit back with my green t-shirt on, kick back, and think about how I got up, out of bed that second day,—it was 7:00 A.M. I had breakfast, then afterwards I/we ended up standing in a formation, all 400-of us, for there was a second flight [plane] that came in the same evening ours came in, although a little later. In any case we all stood in this large horse-shoe three-quarter circle. The Command Sergeant Major, a First Sergeant, and a Major were present;—along with a Master Sergeant [E-7] who did the talking. Then he started calling names,

he said, with a stern voice [the Master Sergeant]:

"The next seven names are going to be infantry," adding an even more aggressive and dominate tone to the demand,

"…and I don't care what your MOS is [job title], you have two occupations, one is what you are trained to do, and the second is infantry [also what we are trained to do], and we are short of infantry."

He was right, we were trained usually in one area, and the infantry side was the killing training, which everyone got the same dose of. The good point was they didn't call my name for the infantry. Now there were three of us left, and the sergeant said,

[With a warning emphasis.] "You three will stay here,"—strange how things happen, I whispered under my breath. This was not democracy, but it worked. I had said under my breath again, in the heat of the morning, '…it was a prayer…' I was not used to praying, but I did say, 'Lord, I wish I'd stay right here…' and I did. Not sure why I liked it, because I didn't know a thing about where I was, but it seemed like home,—anyplace would have felt that way I suppose but I have learned "…ask and you shall receive…," Matthew 7:7 New Testament. I was not

25

a religious person back then, but I knew of him, maybe that was good enough, you know, like the preachers say: just a little faith moves mountains.

5

The Bomb

[And the toe]

I had hurt my right leg [foot really] in Germany, by having a bomb fall on it, an eight-inch projectile [about 200-lbs of weight]; it smashed my toes to hell on my right foot, and so I limped a little, shifting about fourteen-pounds of my weight to my left side. I was not a good runner anymore. And while taking jungle training in Washington State, I was getting a medical deferment for [or put another way,—from] going to Vietnam because I wouldn't be able to run like the rest of the soldiers, when I most needed to, I suppose they felt. But back then I was a restless kind of guy, which I still carry with me to this day [the restlessness that is]; but on the other hand, needless to say, I ended up in Vietnam none the less. Let me explain.

I jumped on the jet going to Vietnam without seeing the doctor, or waiting for the deferment;—why, there we go again, that restlessness. When I got to Vietnam and went through the assignment process, the medics, after checking me for what they called a 'basic-check up' upon entering the country, then started to check my medical records, asked

[unenthusiastically—wiping his forehead from the sweat] "…why are you not in the hospital at Fort Lewis PFC Evens?" [He showed my medical records and what was indicated in it which was to be examined by a foot specialist].

I said, with a squeaky kind of voice, I think:

"My appointment was for Thursday, and the plane was leaving Tuesday." They looked at me strange as if I left out something. So I added,

[Quickly.] "I got fed up." The medic looked at me, shock his head,

"I'm from Alabama," [He pronounced the a like in random]. "And we're not that dumb down there." Then gave me a half smile, and laughed a bit, looking at his friend [his friend sitting by his side that is] who shook his head, not knowing if to cry, or laugh because of how I approached life I suppose,

and said,

27

said that [the assisting medic],

"You're here now buddy and you're not going back,—no-p Uncle Sam is not paying for a round-trip ticket yet, you are not going back, not right now. Sor-rrrrryyy-i-e!"

[I understood the first time he really didn't need to repeat it, I think he was thinking I was going to ask to go home but I didn't] I commented,

[And I was being truthful] "It doesn't matter one way or the other to me." He all of a sudden got frog eyes, big as big can be.

In most cases, I cared more about where I was going to get my next beer more than if I could skip the war and go home. Needless to say [but I will anyways] I was not a married man,—I was free as a bird in a tree; I loved traveling, and war was part of being a soldier, and traveling was also, and so I said to my brain, let's go, no big thing. It was not crazy talk, just a pinch of reality. I promised myself one thing in Vietnam though, I would not go back in pieces, and whoever was in front of me would go down with me, and that seemed fair enough.

And so I told myself with an assuring look, 'I'll simple make the best of it.' [And I did.] I had learned people do not make fun for you, you do it yourself. And if you want life to be hard, life can accommodate that also. I was here for a mission, and I'd do the best I could with what I had, now. I felt it was a simple philosophy, for a simple man.

Tommy the Coke Man

We all had jungle camouflage fatigues—along with boots that were specially made for this kind of terrain and weather. We got old newspapers from back in the states [but as I said they were way out dated by the time we got them] along with the 'Stars and the Strips' [the military version of a large newspaper that was sent out to all military unites wherever US Armed Forces were]; from all sides of the world Vietnam was much in the news; yet after being in this country a while I realized people back home were given only light sketches of reality of the soldier in Vietnam [such as would be the bombing of the tri-ammo dumps here in Cam Ranh Bay].

Tommy, a Specialist Five, like a Sergeant, worked for the mess hall. Like me, he often just wore t-shirts, and was in the base camp most of the time. He was a large man, both tall and wide. Not as strong looking as the Crusher in the company [a person I'd get in a fight with], but none-the-less, no one to want to mess with if you didn't have to. About 230-lbs, 5'll. In any case, he used to sell pop [soda] to us—GI's [soldiers] at the 611th

^{Ordnance Company.} He was one of the few who had a refrigerator [although I acquire one about four months prior to my leaving, and often the electricity would go out leaving the pop warm anyways, not sure if it was worth it.] In any event, he used to sell the pop for .25 cents to anyone in the company wanting it, and sometimes gave credit. He told me once he made $900 in a month. Told me to hush that up, "People get envious you know Chick, be quiet about it…" Well he got that right, people do, especially when they are in need of dope [and to me I had put all drugs, other than alcohol related substances, into one category, being dope] and we had our share of folks with that issue.

He didn't wear a hat for the most part [as I most of the time did], no hat in this region, in this region of the world that is, could be fatal. Yet, and I say yet, lightly—if I was to call him odd, meaning, a bit eccentric in my world, then I'd just as well have to call myself odd, for I was on such a cutting edge if there is one. I suppose [if someone was to give me a nick name it might have been 'Trigger-happy'] my trigger-happy hand, was considered in such a class, everyone told me about my oddity, I was too paranoid.

6

The Last Fight

[And the Thief]

"The Last Fight," not sure why I called it that [for there were a couple of fights in Vietnam I had, before and after this one], but this one had its moments; and the karate I had learned in San Francisco would come in handy, very, very handy. I had thought of saving my energy for the enemy, but trouble in those days seemed to find me no matter where I went, and the company area with my fellow GI—comrades, took the best out of me. Meaning, sometimes your own comrades were more dangerous than the enemy. Having said that let me explain:

I called him the Crusher [as I had previously noted]—I called him that because he had a few fights in Vietnam with other GI's, and I watched a couple of those fights, where he, the Crusher was involved, and he was mean looking just like the wrestler back home called the Crusher.

✳

One night a black soldier [this is another fight, not the one with the Crusher yet] tried to steal some of my things to sell them for drugs/dope, if you will. I always slept with one eye open in those days—believe it or not. His shadow that night, as he crept in, and around my bed, his shadow crossed my eyes…just a little draft came with it, as he turned around starting to—to go the other way, back where he came from;—I jumped over my boxes, several that made a barricade to the side of my bed, thus, one had to go around it to get to me,—I jumped right over and onto the shadow, with my one open eye, it was about 3:00 AM. I beat the shit out of the man-shadow, [he was a black soldier] as his buddy stood there watching, both high on dope—then they both ran,—I picked up my merchandise he had stole and dropped when I landed on him; his friend was simply 'a

30

watch person':—watching to see who would come in or out of the hut, while the theft was taking place. They really never expected me to wake up. They were looking for things to sell to buy dope with.

The hutch was not much to speak of, four walls, and a door to close, but it was home, away from home. And there was not much room. By and large we all had the same amount of room, [or space, square footage if you will]. And although we woke up everyone, and the two blacks ran,—it's funny no one came to my rescue. I think everyone wanted to keep out of everyone else's affairs. But then on the other side of the coin, everyone was on something most of the time. Thank god it wasn't Charlie [the enemy whose shadow I jumped on].

The following morning the other black soldiers were wondering if I was going to go to the Captain [I could tell this by the looks I was getting], but I didn't…—it was an internal thing I felt, and he [the black robber] was no more than a wasted dope freak. He would eventually get short [his time would run out for being in the Army], and instead of leaving Vietnam and going home, he'd choose to go and live in the village of all places, hung up on that white shit, heroin. He is probably still there [as this story is being written], or dead.

When I took my shower the following morning [after I beat the shit out of the thief] I felt this was it, a new battle brewing, several blacks approaching me. I stood in the shower with the water running over my back [adopting an equally to the point manner]. But what they simply said was [standing beside the wooden shower house:

"Look, there's mighty mouse [then switching the subject as they walked away]." I was a quiet soldier for the most part [quiet in the sense I kept to myself], and surprised them, I think with my hands on approach in defending my territory, it shocked them. Plus I had a few black friends of my own; and back then the blacks and whites pretty much kept to themselves, except for me I suppose, I didn't realize, nor did it occur to me there might be racial, if not radical issues floating in the air in the racial area. And I'm sure they asked my black friends, and were told I was ok, for being a white guy. Back then, the blacks as well as whites had clinches; in any event, I was the victim, and had done a few favors for a few of my black friends, as they had for me. And so a simple monologue was expressed and they went on their way.

One of my black friends, a Buck-Sergeant, let me use his beautiful leather shoes for R&R [Rest and Recuperation] in Sidney, Australia. Hold your horses—[I'm getting back to the Crusher in a moment]. He was most likely one of my supporters in this theft vs. fight.

Anyway, the enemy was not always the VC [Viet Cong], as you can see. Matter of fact, even though they would sneak into our camp, set up a few traps, liked putting a bullet behind our hutch doors, so when you closed them a small gun shot noise would go off, just enough to scare you. But that was nothing compared to the Military Police, next door to our compound, who were camped beside us, who caused us a little trouble, and we retaliated by throwing a grenade into their camp one night, and blew up the whole movie screen. Things got a little out of hand now and then;—the things no one much hears about.

The Crusher

As I was about to say, I lived in St. Paul, Minnesota, and used to go to see the wrestling matches downtown at the Armory [mid-1960's], and once the wrestler, called the Crusher, walked down the isle to the ring, he walked a foot from me, right past me, I'll never forget that, not a hero, but surely a good entertainer, and a sight to behold, he was muscle, muscle and strength. Anyhow, people were trying to touch him, in particular, one guy was trying to push him, etc., and actually touched him in the process,—the Crusher took one hand and shoved the annoying spectator backwards off and over the stool he had behind him; one sweep, that's all it took just one quick sweep, and the guy went flying like a fly. As he fell back, he landed on his arm;—no problem, I think the guy liked it.

In any case, my sergeant friend looked like the Crusher, and I say friend loosely, for he was quite boastful. He was an infantry man, and had spent a few times, long periods of time [s] that is—in the jungle. He was starting to loose mentally it seemed, so whatever company he was assigned to, prior to coming to the 611th, for they sent him to us, he was not to go back until he got mentally stable. For the most part, it was long term jungle fatigue. As I was saying, he was assigned to our Ordnance Company to assist with the supplying of arms to other units throughout the area, and would have to do so, until he gained his sanity back. He did although his share of work along with his share of drinking, and was for the most part a bully.

He could be a good sort of fellow at times though, when he wanted to be, when he was sober that is, but the other part of him was strange and mean, boastful, quickly offended. He liked Vietnam, or so it seemed, for he never came out and told me so, and he liked killing I think, again a conjecture, but befitting. Once he took my taller friend Bruce, I being five feet eight inches, and him five feet eleven, and the Crusher being about six foot-one, and pinned Bruce against the wall in our hutch, right by my bed, and hit him several times——he fell to the floor like a paper bag. He was half snapped though [drunk].

Bruce's bed was across from mine, and the Crusher's was in back of mine, in an enclosed area [his being the only enclosed room in the hutch], being the ranking man. The sergeant, that is, the Crusher, looked at me, and around the hutch, as if to say: I got some more of this for anyone who would like some,—kind of bragging, and provoking almost, hoping someone would say something [all remained quiet]. I told myself I'd be ready for him because somewhere along the line he was going to try and beat the shit out of me, just a matter of time I told myself. I knew the day was coming though; I have good senses if anything. Apart, from my Irish-Russian temper I could surely get in the way somewhere along the line with the Crusher, and could even provoke him, and should I annoy him along these lines by not obeying his every wish [my temper that is could get in the way], I would not be as easy taken down as Bruce was, I assured myself of that.

Bruce was the sergeant in the orderly room, who did assignments for everyone, and I guess he did the Crusher wrong on a few occasions, such as not giving him leave, but Bruce did everyone wrong, and he surely had it coming. But what a mismatch, I mean the Crusher had muscles coming out of his nose; his arms were as big as my thighs. He was like a bull if anything. How would you fight a guy like this? And when he got drunk, and mad, boy oh boy, you couldn't hurt the demon inside of him I'm sure. Or so I thought, evaluating the situation that evening when Bruce got it.

Well, we lived in what we called this hutch [short for wooden and tin cage], four men to the place;—again, the Crusher was a sergeant, and I was a corporal. And so he got the enclosed sleeping room, as I have already mentioned. When a friend of mine left, he gave me his outside antenna, and so I made sure it was hooked up to the top of the hutch, getting Saigon's transmission at night; I had also bought the person's TV, which was quite the commodity in Vietnam, if only you could get good enough reception the TV would be worth having, although you only got an hour or three of reception-time, and it was mostly news.

Well, the Crusher saw my antenna hooked up on top of the hutch, and that I got good results with it by checking out my TV, as he walked daily though the front door of the hutch, and put his wiring on to mine [when I wasn't around] so he could also get good transmission, for he had just purchased a TV from a GI leaving, like me. Again, we only had a few hours a night of TV reception, and mostly it was all news, but what the heck, it was a distraction. In spite of it all, I took it off [his antenna]. His sergeant friend, George, who had a Vietnamese girl-friend, and was fighting with her and trying to make an agreement with her not to fuck anyone [everyone] while he was on leave, for he was about to go on leave shortly,—going home to see whoever, probably his other girlfriend. Well, he came to me and told me the Crusher didn't like the idea I had taken his wiring off my antenna and to watch out especially if he got drunk he'd take it out on me. I told him to go tell his Sergeant friend, who was in the room about ten feet away from me 'it stays off,' the antenna that is, and he could see me about it if it bothered him.

✳

However, it was about three days later, about 9:00 PM at night, when the matter came up again. He was drunk, and he came to me and said he wanted to talk to me in his little room, and so I went in it. He put it to me quite bluntly, saying [appalled at my actions]:

"You best put the wiring back on or I'm going to nail your ass to the wall..." I said no. His sergeant friend [George] stayed outside of the enclosed room within the hutch, with my black friend Terry, a sergeant who was to borrow me his shoes for my R & R [Rest and Recuperation] trip to Australia coming up. I could hear them talking. I think Bruce was telling Terry, I told Chick, now he's going to get it. If I knew Terry, he'd had said nothing, and I couldn't hear him, so most likely he didn't, and was simply awaiting the fight, because if anything, he knew I was a little crazy, or possible just as crazy as the Crusher.

As I looked at the Crusher [swallowing, and clearing my mouth, as if to clear my throat also to prepare for battle], I told him it wasn't his wire, and he was fucken rude, and if he wanted to ask in a nice way, I could be persuaded to let him use it. I tried to speak in a tone of voice I would call 'quiet humor'—, that is, trying to defuse the situation.

I said [hesitating] "Ask, don't assume you can use what doesn't belong to you." Outrage came in this man's face [the man called the Crusher] He now was not responding and now we both had a silent glare–staring at each other's face, as if we were not close enough,—our faces seemed to stretch forward. [He was a beast, bully and fool, and I do not use the word 'fool' lightly.] He was thinking—without infinitesimally, only with misplaced emotion.

"Fuck you and your nice way..." he told me point-blank. I started to turn around, I said, blatantly:

"Have it your own way, but don't put it back up, I'll just take it back down." I knew as I was making my turn he was going to try and start tossing me about in that little room, and the room was way too small for a fight. And he was getting madder, redder and stuttering with not knowing what to say. I went for the door, his shadow moved,

"Stop," said the 210-pound sergeant turning [it was the tone, not the words that said to me, that I recognized, it was that of battle, no less]. My 165 pounds, pretty solid poundage, and fast with my fists, and I had three years of karate backing me up, I saw him become reckless with his open posture.

"Ah," he said, "Yes I see you now a little waking up boy!" Now he stopped, "I'm from the jungle where all the action is, you're just a support nobody," he spit out with carelessness.

[Modestly] "But without us 'support nobodies,' how would you been able to kill those little Vietcong-gook soldiers?...matter of fact, how come they sent you back, too much for the big man out there?" [Now I was getting mad and mocking.]

That was it, I put salt on a wound, not sure what wound that was, except he was sent back for mental and fatigue rest [or so I was told].

"I warned yu," he said, "That's not good enough?" I noticed the dim light in his room...............

His head was huge, a good size stomach also, a wide face and large hands; he now stood about five inches from my face.

"You better change your mind Corporal, or I'm going to pound your fucken head in!"

Aggravatingly I commented, with a half smile: "Start pounding," adding, "It's still no, and that's the way it is."

He pulled his hand back as if to cock it like a gun, preparing to hit me, actually expecting me to allow him to do so without doing anything [like he did to Bruce], but I surprised him; I blocked his power punch, and shoved him back onto his bed, he fell backwards lost his balance, like a hippo. I could have jumped on him, but I thought that wouldn't do a thing, I needed room;—as that thought faded the war between him and I had started............ŒΣw

....

........................wwwwwwwwww the sound of war was was, every where...

"Mother fucker, mother fucker, I'm going to kick the shit out you; just wait fuck head..." He was slurring his speech, and I think I was also, both a little drunk. I didn't swear, which was really normal for me, I just said, "Yaw, yaw..." keeping my cool, as I was taught in San Francisco, by my master instructor, Gosei Yamaguchi.

He looked up at me, and then looked at the door; he knew he was in a vulnerable position.

"Let's go outside by the hutch," he demanded.

As I opened the door and walked out, Bruce stood there dumbfounded. I commented, "Just stay where you're Bruce, we don't need an audience, and you too George."

The Crusher came out, roaring and swearing and we both ended up on the boardwalk outside the hutch

there were three others looking at us, his friend in disbelief, surprised I was still alive as I looked in the entrance way, the light of the inside hutch shinning on him, and then I noticed it was raining a bit, and so within a few seconds, the Crusher joined me,—he started to throw rights and left punches. I blocked everything he threw; he was madder than a hornet, he couldn't hit me though [mad as a hornet, huge like a hippo, and slow as a turtle]. Almost shaking his head, and getting tired of trying, he went to grab me and I broke his hold onto my arm and shoulder, then I kicked him in the groin with my knee, but he kept on coming. He was like a train charging through a barrier.

I was not getting tired yet, and wanted to fight a closer fight. I had fought taller men before, and one of the main things is to get close, the reason being, they need room to stretch their long arms and legs,—so I moved in, which prevented him from cocking his fists, or getting a punch in on me,—every time he tried, I'd hit his arms, throw them to the left and right, almost putting him off balance, and with all that weight he carried on him, it wasn't too hard to get him off balance, it was just hard to block his solid heavy arms as they came crushing forward for a knock out punch; unknowingly, he left me several openings; I gave him elbows under his arms to the ribs, punches and kicks, but nothing would put this guy down, yet he was getting tired. I don't think he ever hit me once.

Then getting frustrated on what to do with this guy, I twisted my body like a spiral, stepping back two feet, knowing he would come forward any second, which he had already started to, I jumped in the air, when I came down, I took my fingers and planted them into his forehead, and scraped all the way down and over his face to his neck; I had long fingernails back then, just for such occasions. When I landed his face was all blood. I had put such deep groves into his face he screamed and stepped back. Now we both were looking at one another.

Bruce said,

"Let's stop here, we're all going to get in trouble," meaning a Non-commission officer, the Crusher, was fighting a corporal, [me] a less grade, or rank, or enlisted man; this was grounds for an undesirable discharge, or Court Marshal for him. Plus, he threw the first punch in and outside the hutch. And so I walked in the hutch, and the Crusher walked behind me. When we got in, he grabbed me and threw me against the wooden wall. Before he could come any closer, I jumped into a stanza position.

"I thought it was over," I said, as he went to grab me and try to throw me against the wall again, but this time I got in a solid stance [as if my feet were plastered to the floor] and egged him on [but this time he was more careful, he didn't rush me in fear I might know or do something he'd regret],

"Ok, you want it, come and get some more, big boy;" now they were holding me back and him [that is, George and Bruce were holding me, and two other GI's were holding the Crusher]. I figured the only way to put this hippo down was to go for a kill blow, but god forbid if it worked, under his arm pit, I could puncture his lungs, or I could go for driving his nose bone up into his spine or break an arm and hope that would stop him. I guess it came down to whatever my mind said at the last second, and if he charged me, and gave me an opening.

Bruce said, in a preachers tone:

"The First Sergeant's coming, we can all get in trouble for letting this fight go on," he repeated himself sternly.

Everyone started leaving and the Crusher and I stood looking at each other for a moment, and then went to our living spaces. Bruce and George went into the enclosed room, with the Crusher.

We both needed to cool off,—to carry this any further was really not needed,—our tempers got wild, when least expected—we both had come to this conclusion I believe; yet in a way I kind of was glad it happened, get it over with. I had sensed for a long while he took a dislike to me, or if not that, at least in some way I did not look up to him, and it bothered him; but then I didn't look up to many people in those days.

His friend George came back the next day and asked if I was going to press charges on the sergeant for him hitting a lower ranking GI. I said I had no reason to.

Then he said, with a soft arrogant voice:

"You know his face looks bad, he said you fight dirty, like a woman…sort of. And if you want to continue with the fight he is willing."

I said back to him [lightly offended],

"First of all, I doubt a woman can twist her body and jump in the air high enough to leave marks like that in his face, and second, there are no rules in fighting, if that was the case he out weights me by 100-pounds, and is four inches taller than me. Who is doing the cheating here? Go back and tell him, I don't want to fight anymore, but if he thinks he can push me around, he knows where I sleep: I'll fight him everyday of the week if that is what it takes to satisfy him. Plus, fighting dirty, what's that, something you made up?"

I added, "He just doesn't like that he can't push me around like he does everyone else."

George commented [arrogantly], "You know he can take you?" I knew he was trying to start something then. Why didn't he say, 'I know I can take you,' and fight me instead of having his friend who wasn't there be the recipient of his wish-list.

I replied [and didn't give him much to bring back to the Crusher], "Maybe he can, but that is not the issue with me. The issue is, I will not be pushed around by him or for that matter, anyone, and if need be we can/or will have to fight everyday, as I already said, and that is that."

Well, it must have worked, he never bothered me again. But for a few weeks he gave me some stares, bad looks, edgewise looks of contempt, almost as if to say, "I wish you would start something." And my looks said, "You know where I sleep." For the most part, I tried not to look at him; I had other things on my mind. So often people think they possessed every thought of your time, when in essence they don't, plus I didn't let it. I figured if he wanted to go through the ordeal again, he'd get drunk one night and start it back up. But that never happened. Incidentally, he never did ask to attach his wiring to my antenna after that, but had George ask about a week later, nicely, and I said, "Yes, it was fine with me." And that was that.

7

Rockets at the Ammo Dump

[Where the Birds Don't Sing]

The rockets were coming all around us, and within the ammo dumps grounds, I was in the middle of it all,—this was the first time I had ever seen Commission Officers of every rank running and hiding like mice running from cats, and high ranking sergeants doing the same; soldiers digging holes in the dirt so not to get their bodies torn apart from the scrap metal [shrapnel] flying all about. Three rockets hit, one behind the headquarters hut, more like a shack, another by the water tank, and one by the five-ton-truck that was suppose to take me back to base camp, every time they hit, I had breakfast in my hands [and I counted three times]; that is, I'd be climbing up onto the back of the five-ton-truck, just before I got onto the trucks platform wanting to get to one of the wooden seats on each side of the truck to finish my breakfast], a rocket came. I could hear the rocket's whistle-at times a humming sound; its velocity had that stunning and almost paralyzing tone; a twisting velocity sound that went right to the marrow of your bones. I ended up throwing my breakfast in the air ALL THREE TIMES, jumping to the ground some several feet down, and finding a place to hide.

This was not the first time rockets came in and around where I was, but it was nonstop and oncoming this morning more so than usual, as if they had zeroed in on this particular location, right where all the Officers [brass], and sergeants were. [I would find out later, that it made the newspapers in Vietnam and back home, in either case, they indicated 50% of the tri-ammo dumps were destroyed in this area, by and large, the paper really toned-down the journalistic-truth of the matter].

During the first hit [bombardment of rockets], I hid under a truck; the second, I jumped off the truck, and under the water tank, which was about 15-feet to the left of me, I was thinking the truck might get hit, since the rocket came pretty close last time, which was about ten-minutes ago; the Viet Cong [enemy] had us zeroed in within a radius of a square block. Each time I heard the sounds

39

of the incoming rocket, I stood still for a moment checking out, or trying to, in what direction it was coming, it was like a bee getting louder, and louder, everyone reacting differently, I looked about amazed; yet, it was becoming old news, that is,—after hearing the first whittlings of the incoming rockets, then the explosions, I kept my cool. No need to over react I told myself.

I didn't realize at the moment, [but I do now] I could actually pin-point which direction the rockets were coming, and I did, and I hollered out which direction to the hundred or so soldiers standing around.

You're never sure, that is to say, you never quite know if you are able to react properly, and promptly,—not until the first time has passed, thus, moving in the right direction and keeping focus is the main objective I learned quick. In such a moment a gun or rifle is useless. But you learn swiftly in this war you needed to know how your mind and body would react, or at least I did, by knowing this you knew when to stand, run, hide, listen; in essence, how to react so you didn't run into harms way. Matter of fact, today, as well as two other times being under attack, I was becoming aware of many things, one being I'd leave this war in one piece, or a lot of the gooks [Viet Cong] would go down with me.

That's what we called them, yes, a dehumanizing name, not sure what they called us, maybe round-eyes, or worse, but I would guess it was not the *Great American Boys*. In any event, they like us, had to kill and to kill you had to dehumanize; it's part of the preparation for taking a life. That is what Uncle Sam teaches you, trains and pays you for, to be a killer. What else in the long run is a soldier good for. It is like an accountant with no numbers to deal with, what good is she or he good for. You can use them as you will, but when you need them, they got to know accounting; like a soldier, he has to know how to kill. [Or be killed. Not much gray in this area.] In essence, no matter how you looked at it, one had to be ready. But again, I learned keeping my cool was something that came automatically, thank god.

I had wanted to get the hell out of here on the truck and back to base camp [several times], I was tired and hungry. I had been out all night long, eleven of us out of 169-soldiers in our company. We got hit last night, and for some reason, the rest of the soldiers were not able to function properly, some out of heroin usage, others on pot [in essence, a high majority on drugs] and still others passed out on booze [alcohol]. And so there were just us 11-soldiers available, 'what a joke' I told myself.

I had my share of beer the night before, but I was ok, my sensory-perception seemed to be 70% effective; I was aware of all movements about me. We got hit bad last night, and I went out along with a squad into the dark empty unguarded ammo dump to secure it, thinking Charlie [the enemy] would infiltrate it.

✳

As I stood by the truck again [for the umpteenth time], thinking this morning it was all over as far as incoming rockets were concerned, I heard the sound of the humming-bee again, getting closer and closer,

"Oh shit," I said [hoarsely], "…the whistling, another damn rocket."

I looked about, no place to hide. There was the Colonel, he was running like a jack rabbit, and the sergeant who talked a good battle while sitting in the wooden shack-office day after day counting the stock in the ammo dump, and for the most part, wasn't all talk, he too was running, and the Major, the Captain, and all the privates. I jumped along side of a thirty-foot embankment. Somehow I missed it before, 'where was it,' my mind asked my eyes [?] A rhetorical question at best, for it gave no answer only curiosity itself. I asked myself, it's better and safer than the damn truck half full of gas, or the water tank that could have collapse on me had it got hit, and a few thousand pounds on my frame, this was less vulnerable; but there it was, a short distance from the lopsided wooden headquarters shack,—the things you miss when the shit hits the fan. This shack or command station in the ammo dump was really our home base, away from home, which was the camp several miles away [which was about three-miles down the road, and four-miles along the coast of the South China Sea, and about two miles inland from the peninsula].

I had my rifle in my hand now, my helmet was still on my head, it fell off twice before when I was running and jumping for shelter. Another sound——a whistle was coming in closer; another bee I told myself. As I turned my head around to look down the thirty-foot embankment to the people on the ground below me, several were digging holes in the ground like ground-hogs; others looked like dogs digging for bones, they hid their faces, throwing dirt on their backs, waiting and hoping the metal fragments, when they started to fly, would miss them, or if not miss them, at least miss their faces.

The whistling-sound of the rocket [one rocket this time] was getting closer and closer. I peeked--slowly—above the embankment, to my left,—in the best sense of the word, there was my 'homey' [my friend from my home town], yes, it was him, standing frozen by the guardhouse. Why he didn't move was beyond me [I told myself]. But then I had seen it before, you freeze sometimes in such situations.

"Move, MOVE, in coming!" I yelled.

He didn't move, but he caught my eyes. The sound was getting closer, I looked in the sky, you can't see those rockets coming, just hear the whistling-sound [the humming coming from the twisting velocity of the projectile] as they approach, closer and closer;—and these are multi-seconds I am talking about some times,—not minutes, but things happen that quickly in war.

"Mooooooooooove…" I yelled again

I had no choice' I pulled my head back, covered it with my forearms and helmet, and waited for the sound, the explosion. I think I heard a thump, yes, that's what I heard, nothing else. I stayed put [not moving], then looked [waiting to see if this one round, that is rocket, had a delayed reaction] slowly over the embankment again I looked. The shack was still standing; the truck and water tank was in place. Everyone was hiding, and there was my homey, on his knees, his hands in a prayer position. What happened I asked myself? I looked about again, scanning the whole area, where is the rocket, and then I noticed my homey shaking, just shaking like a loose leaf on a tree. Everything was silent, no birds singing [birds don't like war zones I was learning], no lizards moving, nothing, just silence, as if the clock-of-time had stopped.

My homey moved a little, there, there, I saw something, I started to get up from my position, and the rocket was three feet from him, 'my god,' I said, 'what luck.' He looked at me as if he was frozen with fear, afraid to take his hands out of the prayer position, in fear that is, the rocket would go off. His eyes were the only things moving on his body.

As I got up on my feet and started to walk towards him, many of my comrades came out of their hiding places, and then I saw the rocket [the one that I heard the whistling coming from, but no explosion] about eight-inches into the dirt.

"I'll be damn, it didn't go off, it didn't go off, it didn't go off…" I repeated to myself several more times; prayers must work I concluded, for this was surely a miracle. I stood erect, walking closer to my homey, it was to his right [the rocket that is].

When I got to him, I asked if he was ok, he started to stutter, I knew he wasn't ok, and wouldn't be for a very long time. The medics came, walked him over to the truck, I jumped on the back of it, he was in the front seat with the driver, and medic. We went back to base camp. I felt good on one hand to get the hell out of there, I had been there since 1:00 AM last night, and now it was about 10:30 AM; nine and a half hours of dodging scrap-metal, rockets, and this was my third victory over death, not including the nighttime.

When we got back to the company area, my friend was taken to the clinic where in about three days they took him to Japan for medical treatment. [Seven months later I ended up going home. And about 18-months after that, I called him up, he told me he couldn't talk or see me anymore; I was part of his memory, a part that triggered the elusive moment when the rocket froze along side of him, where time stopped. He asked me not to take it personal;—it was simply too much for him. And so I honored his request, and after thirty-five years, I have yet to call him, nor will I; he was a good soldier, and a lucky one.]

8

Engagements

[Other Activities]

I had worked eight-hours that following day, got about three hours sleep, then nine-hours in the field of dreams, dodging the rockets, and once back to base camp, I had three more hours sleep, and had to go back to work. I had at this point left out the evening conflicts [prior to my homey getting frozen, and the rocket not going off, so I will now], but I was asked, thereafter [about two weeks later] if I would accept an *Army Commendation Medal for Valor*. I refused it on the grounds, my 'homey' [person from my home town, in this case he was a relative of a friend of mine back in the neighborhood who I used to hang out with] should get it, not me, but I did accept a metal for extra ordinary service, for that evening, and morning conflict. But I should add that that evening conflict was even scarier than the following morning bombardment. Let me explain:

✳

One man died, three ammo dumps were targeted and bombed and blown all over the area, and for some odd reason, Delta, the dump I was in, got only the incoming shrapnel which was flying all about from the Air Force Dump [other than receiving incoming, the enemy only hit dirt at Delta dump, Charlie dump was emptied out, which was next to our dump, but the papers would read, 50% of all three dumps were demolished, this was not true; although 50% if not more of the Air Force dump was]; the shrapnel went as far as the South China Sea, three to four miles away—yet the dump was but a few miles from me/us [the Air Force dump].

The evening was horrific, deadly.

44

A huge hot red piece of metal [about the size of my fist] flew by my face that evening [2:45 AM], about one, maybe two inches from my face. I told a soldier, who was suppose to be guarding a part of the dump to the south of me, but wasn't because he was standing by me talking like a manic-fool [haphazardly], who was falling to pieces [in the sense of mentally that is];—in point of fact, I told him he was not in his proper location, guarding and insuring the enemy did not infiltrate the south area, accordingly, endangering lives, if not me, himself.

He was scared to death, I tried to calm him down, and told him to get himself together [more shrapnel was flaying by us, all about];—we being only eleven that evening out of 169-soldiers—we needed all the eyes we could get to insure the area was free of the enemy; watching him tremble made me nervous, and just standing there was dangerous, I repeated to him,

"What are you doing here; get the fuck back to your location before we both get killed."

"I can't. I don't know what to do, where to go," he said with a tear in his throat, as if I was going to abandon him.

I said,

"Just go back to your location, secure it, and make sure no VC gets in."

He replied with reeking anxiety throughout his whole body,

"Secure what, we're being blown apart all over the place." Well, he was right, but none-the-less, we were here and we needed to remain for the time being, you can't really guard anything when you are being rocketed, and so on, not very well anyways. The main point was, was that we couldn't go back to base camp, we were stuck right here, and we had to be here, and therefore, protect ourselves until it was over. Survive the moment.

He did then return to his post south of me, I told him to transverse when he run, less of a chance to get hit.

As the night went on he came back to me wondering aimlessly again, asking what to do after the Air Force ammo dump went up in flames [everything was being hit, all three dumps]; the explosion was so powerful, it shook the whole foundation of the area.

I got thinking, was he in shock [?]——Or simply fear and disbelief,—as you looked up into the night sky, the overhead was a mushroom; it looked like an atomic explosion had taken place.

Here is this man wanting to talk, with flying metal all about. I told him to get to an embankment again, to stop walking around and wanting to talk like a fool, that he was a dead man if he didn't wake up. Scrap-metal was flying by our faces again, at one point he was going into hysterics, the scrap metal went by my face missing it by an inch this time,—it was a heavy solid square piece of red hot iron,—he saw it as the velocity and the sound of the hissing hot metal filled his ears, he leaned over as if to puke; I told him at that point,

"Get the fuck out of here now," [meaning he needed to move and so did I before more scrap-metal came flying by]; in consequence, he ran south again, as I was running up a hill to the right of me, another big explosion went off, and I flew in the air some fifteen feet:—when I landed my rifle went two feet into the mud, it had started to rain out that evening off and on. Actually that was good in the sense it helped put out the fires at the Air Force dump.

On another note, we were pretty lucky, because we had three dumps in the vicinity. The one I was in, Delta dump, which was full of arms, and Charlie dump, which was emptied out just a few weeks ago, and its ammo put into Delta, and the Air Force which had high explosives.

Well, when we got rocketed, they hit all three dumps, but mostly Charlie and the Air Force, and nothing was in Charlie Dump, as I had mentioned, we had moved it. So we lucked out really well, except for the three men who got caught in the atrophy at the Air Force dump. When it went up, that is, when the explosions took place, two got out alive, the other didn't make it.

Soldier at the Fence

The attack had gone across the three ammo dumps, throughout the night, and morning, I did make it back to base, and had a good breakfast. In point of fact, several helicopters were called in to hit with arms the Viet Cong Units across the bay that had been shooting rockets over at us, that is over the ammo dump, around the dump, and in the three dumps that rested by one another like a triangle [carelessly shooting rockets that is]: and so they did, and in consequence that was the end of the enemy, and it took the edge off our unit. At that point of time, the tri-ammo-dump's evenings patrols were doubled, especially those areas that were most vulnerable to penetration.

Two Weeks Later

I never knew what day it was unless I looked on the calendar, or for that matter what time, sometimes what month, for it always seemed summer or spring to me over there.

One evening I had guard duty, that evening I was sent out to the dump to guard an area equal to a two square block area, and Tommy my friend, was to the north of me, some four blocks at any given time, for he also had the same amount of area to secure. Again, it was normal to guard the area, but we usually had two patrol men in a jeep making rounds three times a night: not anymore than that, but because of the tension within the Army circles of *Cam Ranh Bay*, the higher ups, and the amount of munitions lost in the previous explosions, at the Air Force Dump, the General wanted more security within the dump areas itself, all night long. Matter-of-fact, it was rather quiet for the past two weeks, and possible that may have contributed to it [us being there 24-7 now].

And so, instead of the eight that normally secured the area, along with the Military Police,—now we had sixteen of our own men guarding the dump, along with twice as many MP's. When we got the duty, it didn't stop our other jobs. We'd get off guard duty and clean up only to go to our other jobs in the morning. Yes, it was a 16-hour day. But heck, it was just part of the fun.

As I walked my post along the fence, the silence almost put me into an estranged mood. I could hear every sound it seemed. The far off trees and bushes with their dark tops, grassy bottoms, harbored many shadows with the few lights we had. In addition I had a flash light, when in need.

The fence between me and the forest was about 100-yards directly west. I had my M16 locked and loaded, carried it barrow down: pacing and thinking, thinking and pacing, thinking, and thinking; it seemed like I never stopped thinking, and I never quite got a good night sleep.

The moon looked a little blood-shot this evening I thought, like the way my eyes looked when I was coming off a good drunk the evening before; although the moon was not real clearly light, but enough to spot any unwanted movements in the distance, and with the fog around it, it radiated some colors, or so it seemed, and I wasn't on anything like drugs, but it was kind of psychedelic, in a manner of speaking. But often nights were like that, you just didn't notice those nights until you were on guard duty alone.

"Who goes there," I challenged. The figure kept on walking; I could hear his feet pushing the wet grass aside, moving the mud,—it had rained the day before, and out in these surroundings things did not dry all that quickly, plus the fog seemed to make everything wet.

"Who are you," I said again, pulling my M16 barrow to my waist level; at the same time I was double checking any movement in the wooded area behind the figure walking. Shadows, shadows, that was all I got, I questioned, mumbling to myself: '…could be Charlie, could be Charlie…' and this man figure showed up,—who knows! I questioned myself.

My partner was too far to the North to assist me so I left that for the lizards, I raised my rifle as if to aim it, and the shadow-figure stopped.

"Private Benson," said the voice, "I'm Private Benson, put down that rifle." I wasn't sure what his motive was for being so far off the beaten track to be here, that was questionable in my mind. Was Charlie behind him, forcing me to show myself so he could shoot me, using him as a shield, who knows I pondered?

"All right, put you hands up where I can see them,—walk to the fence, and grab the fence, NOW!"

He started laughing, I thought this guy was really something, and I didn't have time to play games, so I moved the safety-clip to the off position, downward, so the rifle would be ready for what we called 'rock and roll,' if need be I could spray the whole area behind the figure with bullets. He heard the click of the safety pin move. I figured I had three more magazines [metal cartage holders you put into the M16] fully loaded, in case I needed them.

The Private heard the click of the rifle, and started stuttering, as he saw my weapon being positioned upward from my waist, and starting to be aimed directly at him and my finger was combing the trigger. It's funny when your body is in danger:—your senses are heighten and activated.

As he got to the fence he grabbed it securely, as if to reinforce the fact he was doing as he was told, he had tears in his eyes, he knew he was a breath away from me pulling the trigger. He was a white young lad, about 19-years old, tall, slender and dumb.

"See, I'm a GI like you," he said, in a cocky voice.

"What are you doing out here, setting up something for Charlie?" I commented spartanly, adding, "This area is off limits, and…" he quickly voiced: "I have a girlfriend in the village northwest of here, about a mile."

"You're full of shit; there is no village in this area."

"Oh yes there is, but it only has five shacks, I guess it's not really a village but a number of families live there, I go to see my girl every night, you're the first one to challenge me."

I said with distain,

"Where have you been Private? Last week we almost got blown to hell,—and you're walking like nothing happened.

What unit are you from?"

He had mentioned it, but it went through one ear and out the other, I had not heard of it, then I said, "You mean the radar unit above the hill?"

"Yes, that's the one."

"Well, you know, my unit is right below the hill, the 611th"

With a little more relief in his voice, "Yes, I know your unit is."

—"Show me you're ID card," I requested.

—"Here~!"

I looked at the photo, the Army seal, it was in order.

"Ok, put your hands down, you're free to go, but I suggest you be careful where you're walking, especially drunk."

"Listen Corporal, I feel like I should go to my Commander and let him know how you treated an American soldier."

"Listen Private, at this post I have the power of a General, and don't forget it. You're not a threat and that is why I am allowing you to go, but don't forget I can get you for charges on disrupting my duties. Don't push me."

The private shook his drunken head and walked away from the gate as silly as before.

9

The Truck

[More Engagements]

Barbwire

It brings to mind the first time I got caught under fire. We were on our way to the ammo dump, again to secure it thinking Charlie would sneak in. Three soldiers caught two Viet Cong all tied up in barbwire, they were about three-hundred feet from them [I watched it all from a five ton truck] and they had their M16 rifles aimed directly at them, ready to shoot. One of the men [carelessly] told the other one to call back to base camp to find out what to do. I mean, he didn't know—didn't know really what to do. There were four American soldiers now looking at these two men all tied up [the forth soldier had brought a radio from a jeep to the other three], somewhat cut up in the barbwire were these gooks wondering why they were still alive, why didn't the Americans shoot [how dumb can you be, is most likely what they were thinking]. Would you believe, I told myself—would you believe what you are seeing?

One of the American soldiers said,

"Let's just kill these gooks, get it over with," then the other started fighting with words [aggressively attacking], "We can't, we're American's, and we don't do such things."

I've always been an ambitious sort of soldier—sort of aggressive when need to be, but this was down right dangerous, and would cause some kind of complications down the road I told myself [mark my words, was my way of thinking]

And so they called back to the Captain, who called back to the Major, who tried to get permission from the Colonel. By the time they got back to the four soldiers, the two Viet Cong had gotten through the wire and were on their way up into the surrounding hills. [I told myself, these damn limitations will kill more soldiers. This is what causes one to loose a war. I kept telling myself to calm down, yet I knew these Viet Cong would come back to fight another day]. We are trained to shoot, kill, not this bullshit, I mumbled as the truck took off. They will simply live another day to kill one of us I told the soldiers next to me.

The Truck

As my truck got closer to the Delta Ammo Dump, going down a long dirt road, where it was built up on each side as to create a causeway of sorts,—had we gone too far to the left or right, we'd had be off the man-made-road, and on each side was a cliff, consequently, we'd had been down the cliff also. And so every time I came down this causeway [or land bridge of sorts] I was hoping the driver wasn't high or drunk.

In any event, we now were trying to make it as fast as we could with this five-ton truck, to make up for lost time; down this dirt harden road we went fast and faster, knowing damn well Charlie was up to no good in the hills, and having seen what happened with the four soldiers letting them go, [getting through the fence] we knew we were in trouble, that Charlie had some plans now; if anything a good map and where to hit next. Oh, I could see…Oh—I surely could see something was up, something was in the makings.

It soon became dark, about 9:00 PM; all of a sudden rockets came to the left and right of our truck; explosions and shrapnel became the surrounding scene. The driver stopped, I jumped to the floor [the five-ton truck had an open top]; I was now hiding under my helmet, covering my face. As I noticed the rockets kept coming around the truck, but hitting the bottom of the causeway, I also noticed we were standing still, I look up to see the other eight soldiers frozen to the side of the truck of which they were sitting on the wooden benches provided on each truck for carrying troops back and forth. They had attached themselves to them like 'white on rice'. Then I hollered at the driver:

"They have us zeroed in, get this fucken truck in motion," I knew a moving target was harder to hit, and he froze just like the eight. The rockets stopped for a moment [all the sounds were behind us now], and the truck now was back in motion, going as fast as it could go; I now found my seat among the other eight, I asked:

"Did I do something wrong by jumping to the floor?"

Said the soldier next to me, as everyone else remained silent:

"You're the only one that did it right. We're all lucky we got our heads on our necks yet." A few of the soldiers looked at me, and that was it [no one looked at each other]. To be honest, I wasn't sure if I was right or wrong, but the clarification was good enough for me. I had acted on instinct and how I was trained. I guess I can thank one of those sergeants back at Fort Lewis. Matter of fact, I remember sitting on a bench at Fort Lewis [Jungle Training they called it, prior to going to Vietnam, additional training to the Basic we got at Fort Bragg], and they were going through a map. It was a hot day. Someone asked, "What do you do if you're under rocket fire?" And the sergeant asked several people what they'd do. [Somewhat similar to Quick Fire Training we had in basic, working out of instinct, and automatic reactions] Then he explained, and I did it his way, as simple as it may seem [so whoever you were, God bless you].

10

Free Supplies and the Feud

As everyone did, I also did, mark off the days on my personal calendar. It was a short-timers calendar [meaning when your time got short in Vietnam and you only had days left, not months in the Army, you marked them off, one by one]. But you normally didn't start until you had 30 or 60 days, was the normal rule of thumb. Hell I started at 120-day countdown almost as soon as I got to Vietnam, or so it seemed;—it also seemed more real to me to look forward to marking those days off in the mornings,—that is, before breakfast. But to be quiet honest, what was at home, nothing for the most part, on one hand I didn't care if I marked the days, it was something to do, no more, no less. [But as I may have mentioned, it was a free trip to Asia, and hell, not bad, and I suppose that is where my mind stopped for the meantime.]

Evenings seemed especially dark by my mid-term in Vietnam. It seemed this period many things were happening; not only in and around me, but throughout the world. The Apollo 15 Astronauts, Irwin and Scott took a ride on the moon, with a four wheel moon-rover. Nikita Khrushchev was ill. Papa Doc from Haiti had died, only to hand over his empire of terror to his son Baby Doc, I had not known it then, but I would end up in Haiti, some years down the road. And Bangladesh became established as a new Country; inasmuch as, it really belonged to India [the whole world was changing when I was in Vietnam], and now Pakistan would be another bite taken out of India. The hippie era had come in and was on its way out

yup, here in good old Vietnam, the South Vietnamese troops crossed into Laos trying to cripple Hanoi's supply line along the Ho Chi Minh Trail, for that is where their main road, their life line for supplies were coming down. Yet the VC pushed them back after a while. We lost 89-helicopters, and forty-four American GI's in the ongoing battle of the 'Trail', only to give it back to the takers.

Free Supplies

As I was about to say, the nights were a bit bleak, and we got some scares that Charlie was going to come down out of those holes he made in the mountains and test our skills. If he did, I think we would not have been prepared. Plus he liked getting supplies from our ammo dump. One day a nine-truck convoy came into get supplies from our dump. We supplied the South Vietnamese Army with whatever they wanted. In any case, I was out at the dump that day as our American soldiers were loading the trucks, they never said too much [seemingly, to me a warning emphasis]—they were not as friendly as I was used to experiencing them, one might say,—uneasy, to the point of being on the edge. I mentioned that to a few of the higher ranking sergeants in the ammo dump hut, where they did the paper work, slap flies and do allocations. But they paid little head to me.

"They got the orders, and orders are orders Corporal," they told me.

Well, to make a long and insidious story short and predacious, they, and I say they, for I didn't do it, loaded nine-truck loads of Ammunition for the Viet Cong. It never got into the papers. In any case, we had found out they ambushed the South Vietnamese Soldiers, the ones on our side, took their uniforms, and hurried on up to the dump before it was reported. We got wind of the news about two hours after they had left the area. By that time, they [the Viet Cong] had been long gone, and the trucks with all the ammunition they got free at the ammo dump, by us Americans, had loaded and inventoried for them, were unloaded now. Empty platforms from the trucks were found along with the trucks a few days later in the jungle, empty.

Soldier against Soldier

Along side of the dirt road, yet some three hundred yards separating them, were the two Orderly Rooms for both companies, ours, the Ordnance [Ammunition], and the Military Police's. We were like neighbors that never knew the color of each other's hair. We simply never seem to talk, yet we all spoke the same language. The orderly rooms were small in comparison to the ones in the States, and Germany, which had about 100 square feet in the front, and possible the same to the back section; which half of the back section was the Captains quarters, or office. Our Orderly Room looked identical to the MP's. As you would walk out of the metal-rounded screened-in doors, you stepped out of the office, up about two and a half feet; you were on the dirt road level—where I was standing.

This is just a story of one of the many red-blooded historical scenes that was going on in Vietnam, when we were not fighting or doing something related to war. As one knows, many things are over looked, never said, and often put under the rug. This was one of them. It was soldier against soldier, but then as I often said, I was more worried about my fellow GI's than I was about Charlie, and there is more truth to that than historical-fiction.

Now allow me to get to the Orderly Room event, it was American soldier against American soldier. Captain Bowman was the Military Police's Commanding Officer, even though, we [being] the Ordnance Company, we never got along with the MP's, or him per se [the Captain], we none the less, still heard rumors of the Captain, such things as: he was not all that fair, and was somewhat arrogant; but then many officers were I suppose. I guess he had an extra dose of it, plus he'd go out of his way to antagonize his troops. In Vietnam, we never needed to get haircuts, or shine shoes or for that matter, all we had to do is work, sleep, fight, die, eat, shit, and wake up to start all over again. But Captain Bowman took his Company to a higher level;—spit shinned shoes, and the whole works that go along with state-side duty. It was also hard to get R & R's from him, and Leaves because he never wanted over 10% of his company gone at any given time and his company was only 40% strength to start with, so he would not sign for his men to get 'Rest and Recuperation' although the Captain would allow time off for his soldiers if they wanted to use it for in country leave. So all in all, they had many elements [issues] to deal with and a captain that was on top of you, like white on rice, was not worth his salt, not in Vietnam, and the way the war was being run.

✳

Corporal Thomas, who I never had the pleasure of meeting personally, and probable was lucky to be able to say that, although I had heard his name in passing during several drunken discussions about the MP's, he was a heroin user and trouble maker for the most part and was to become the trying issue of this dilemma, and nightmare, the one that was about to take place in the Military Police [MP] Orderly Room. [I had seen him walking by our Company area a number of times]

As he walked by everyone on this dreary and warm evening, on the roadway just in front of the MP orderly room, I caught a glimpse of him,—he was unkempt, bare footed, armpits stained with sweat, only a green t-shirt on, and some un-ironed jungle-issued-pants. His belt buckle was loose and dangling, and he was unshaven.

By the looks of things, we all thought, that is a few of the fellow's that was with me, he was cleaning his weapon, and was going to the orderly room for some odd reason, possible to see if they had some extra soap they'd give him [maybe that was our wishful thinking, or mine], that they kept on hand for new recruits, or for those who for some reason didn't have any, for it was past normal-duty hours. The CQ [night Sergeant on duty] could get them.

This evening the CQ was there, and the Captain was in his office working late.

Thomas was shaking his head [consoling himself] back and forth, as if he was talking to a ghost or simply talking to himself. His face showed anger mixed with a little hate, he seemed to be spitting as he talked, or it was just slime coming out of his mouth, a finger raised as he walked by as if he was rehearsing for someone to pay attention to him, or even possible for us to stand down, but that last thought didn't come into my head until after the fact.

Whatever he was thinking, he thought he was cleaver, or would be, for the mere fact he was pointing his finger toward his temple slightly to one side as if to gesture intelligence. Again, whatever was on his mind, he had convinced himself he knew what he was doing or about to do.

As he got to the outside of the door, he paced in a circle with his rifle barrel pointed every which way. Now we all started to take note. The CQ came out, we all could see, several of us were standing by the roadway a little in disbelief, or was it shock, not sure.

"Corporal Thomas, what's the problem, do you need something?"

Said Thomas with a little gunk dripping from his bottom lip,

[Now thoroughly resentful—and showing it on his face] "I need to see the Captain, my leave was disapproved."

Said the CQ [emphatically], "Corporal," [Thomas alarmed stares in the CQ's eyes] "He is in–no-oo mood to see you, plus you look too messy, actually you look like shit. Get out of here before he sees you and you get in trouble."

Well, that didn't go over very well, the Corporal looked at the CQ, showed him his fist, with the rifle hanging loose, as if to say you want to fight, then force-fully pushed his punches into the air, he didn't hit the Sergeant, just his fist was clenched, he was like signaling the gods of the air, 'here I come.'

Then he raised his weapon, and the CQ stepping back a foot, looked a little nervous, the Sergeant was clean shaven and you could see his chin from the light over their heads, he thrust his chin towards the Corporal, as if he was meaning some kind of threat, I couldn't hear what was being said. Then the Corporal put the M16-rifle into his belly, and the Sergeant started to rub his chin, as if not to believe what was going on, and shut his mouth. No words needed to be said now.

The sergeant had to do some quick thinking, I was hoping he'd come up with something, we all stood in a trance watching this develop. The sergeant put his palm on his chest, as if to say 'me'. And Thomas told him to leave, and so he did, he came over by us shaking his head and taking in a deep, deep breath;—but not too close to us, I'd say he stood some 20-feet away. And Thomas went through the screen door, right into the Captain's office, several of the MP's now were gathering by the CQ, as he started to explain what had taken place.

Within a matter of minutes, the Captain was being confronted by the Corporal to get off his chair;—then Thomas shoved the Captain in the corner of the two walls behind his desk, we could all see it developing through the Captain's office window.

"How do you like it!" he asked the Captain [pointing his finger at him], with a high ring to his voice.

Adding:

"Can you tell me why the fuck I can't go home?" He pointed his M16 at the Captain's head, the Captain was sweating, and I also noticed, a few tears were rolling down his cheeks, plus it was in his voice [the boarder line of crying]. The only thing I could see on Thomas' face was disgust. He slid his finger under his nose indicating it was too late, and I thought this was it,—the CQ shouted there were several armed MP's out 'here', that if he killed the Captain, he'd die along with him, although I felt, they really didn't want to help the Captain, otherwise they'd had been down there talking to him and trying to persuade him. As I had mentioned, not too many of his own liked him.

Three hours went by,—they kept talking and talking. Then out of the blue, the Corporal came out of the office, gave his weapon to the CQ, and told him to take him to the brig [jail]. However, we didn't have a jail per se on Cam Ranh, but rather what we all called, sweat-boxes, where we kept prisoners. That is to say, metal containers that were about six by nine feet with holes in them used for ventilation and that is what the prisoners lived in and the guards, guarded. We all stood—stood there in amazement [with brows high], not quiet mentally taking all this in, rather storing it to digest later. And that is where he went. It was all hushed up the next morning. And from what I gathered in the passing weeks, he was a much better and watchful captain.

11

The Scorpion

I can't remember all the details, of that particular evening out on patrol in the Ammo-dump, but Charlie was to have penetrated the area, and we were to go find him, seek and destroy. And so when we got to the dump, I lock and loaded my M16, as always. It was about 10:30 PM, and when we finally did a two hours search, found nothing, and was suppose to go back to the company area, our truck was nowhere to be found. We figured the driver and his assistant was getting high, laid or something. So we found some 155-millimeter-rounds to lay against, all crated, others in boxes, and some simply on containers ready to be moved, I lay against those [the wood-crated ammo stock]. There was about seven of us standing around, the others were still doing additional checks for some reason, down to a lower level area;—I think they were bored and didn't want to be found resting for some odd reason, and were doing a double check, it was not called for though.

As I shut my eyes for a moment, my thoughts went all over the place, I actually thought about dying, and came to the conclusion I didn't mind dying then [thinking today might be a good day for it], actually sometimes more so than others I thought like that, today was one of those times I didn't mind.

Smiley, my friend from Alabama, [uneasily], said,

"Don't move…" I opened my eyes, and noticed a scorpion crossing my boots, I was going about to swat him off me, then it occurred to me what Smiley had said, 'Don't,' and then he said again [with a warning emphasis],

"I said don't move, I can get him quicker than you, I've done it before…" He was from the south, and always was making jokes with me about being a Northerner and not knowing about bugs and that kind of crap, but he was right, I didn't know. I noticed he was quite focused on the creature, and so I agreed by nodding my head.

"Don't make a sharp move, "he added. He gave me a five, that is to say, a thumbs up [in the air] meaning, 'ok'. All was in order. So he wanted me to do nothing. I wasn't used to that, but nothing I would do would help at this juncture. Slowly the creature walked up my boots, up to the area of my pants, and Smiley leaned over a little, he knew it had to be soon, for he knew now the creature was going for my warm fabric, not leather, but he was calm and steady, and the back of the scorpion's tail never went up. The scorpion did a side turn and crawled off my boot and pants, I rolled over a little getting out of its way.

"See, no problem...Chick," he [confidently] chuckled a little and I stood up, that was the end of my napping.

12

Vietnam the Country

Much like any other country under the siege of war, South Vietnam back then in the early 70's was no different, that is, it was underdeveloped, lacked good healthy food for its population [yet its Army always seemed to be feed well], to include vegetables and dairy products, and so forth. That is to say, the cities, towns, villages all had shortages of everything, water, electrical power, you name it they had it under a shortage category,—but much like Germany, there was an ongoing black market,—where you could buy anything. If you couldn't find it at the PX, you could at the black market.

As far as we went, the Army that is, we never had hot water up to the 4th month I was there, and then when we got it, it was like a prize, yet in most cases the rain water was warmer, or warm enough, and many of us soldiers just got naked and grabbed a bar of soap and washed in the rain.

On another note, I was good friends with the cooks, and like anyone who had something to offer in trade, they would trade. And so, sometimes I'd go in the back of the mess hall and do my bartering.

Ken the Cook

Ken was 19-years old; he was one of the four main cooks. He happened to have gotten a cute little Vietnamese girl pregnant, and had extended for six more months; it would be his ETS date [meaning, his date to get out of the Army]. He did that for two reasons, one for his girlfriend, for he was confused on the matter of trying to marry her and take her home, and the second was, if he went back to the states with six months to go, where would he go. And so instead of battling the unknown, he stayed put, still as a statue, and when it was time to leave, he'd simply go home.

He came up to me one night and was real puzzled. He brought a few letters from his mother and father, asked me to read them, and so I did. It implied he

60

should not marry the girl of whom he had a child with and simply come home and start his life. That he was much too young to settle down. He asked for my opinion. It was hard to even want to give it, I liked him, but I also liked his small young girlfriend. She was always quite timid, and frail looking, but nice and friendly. She'd had made any man a good wife I think.

Asked Ken [on the verge of tears] "What should I do Chick," worrying of displeasing his parents.

"Do you love her?" I asked, or "…is she just a good time away from home, someone you got pregnant and, oh, well, things happen?"

He said [wide-eyed and stunned], "A little of all that," his voice tiring, as his mind seemed to have gone over it for the hundred time.

"It sounds to me," I said [sarcastically], "As if you have made up your mind to please your parents; or maybe they are making it easy for you to do what you all really want to do."

[Offended] Ken asked,

"And what is that," adding, "…would you—would you mind telling me?"

"A reason to leave her; tell her you will be back to get her and not really come back, or send for her." He looked at me strange,

"Yaw that may be it, is that ok?"

"No," I said, "That is not ok, unless you feel you are at least going to try; plus, you're in Vietnam, in the Army, your parents are not in charge of you anymore. You are not too young to die for your country, and therefore, you are not too young to make a decision. You can't have her waiting for you though, thinking you are coming and you're not. She can find someone else; you're not the only one in the world." Not sure if he liked that or not, but he responded well.

[Optimistically—his tone of voice sounded] "Ok, I'm going to be up front with her and tell her I think it will not work out, that I'm going home and try to figure things out. And no matter what I come up with, I'll always support my child." I smiled, nodded my head, and commented, "Make sure it's your decision, because you'll have to pay for it all your life." He then stood up; we were sitting on the boardwalk across from the mess hall where the hutches were. He had the night shift and went back to work.

*   *   *

New South Wales—City with the Rainbow Door

Sydney, Australia: R & R

When I arrived in Australia, a country plus a continent in itself, I landed in the city called Sydney, which in its own right is in a section of Australia called New South Wales, in comparison:—it might be considered another state, had it been in the United States. Within the city of Sydney I would end up in a hotel in a section of the city called Queensland. And to make my visit a little more geographically complicated,—when I looked from the roof of my hotel you could see the beautiful harbor and a park, I always called it simply, Queen's Park. There were huge trees, a water front, shrubs, flowers: a kind serene wonderland. Yes, the view was meticulously beautiful.

13

Girl from the Farm

[Sydney]

It doesn't seem to matter where you travel, for there is always one thing that stands out among most of the others;—while taking R & R [Rest and Recuperation] in Sydney, for seven days, it was no different [and we'll get to that in a second]. But what made it especially unique, for me anyways, was, it was paid by the US Government, that is, the airfare and my extra seven day leave—and possible the main thing that stood out was the women were much more friendly than the men, or at least to American's and in particular, GI's.

Most all of us GI's in Vietnam got a seven-day R and R to go someplace [such as Hong Kong, Bangkok, Hawaii, or Sydney] even though I had only eight-months to serve, they gave it to me none the less. But back to what I was saying, that you always remember one thing, attached to that female-friendliness was Zolinda a girl I met on a tour. Although I had met quite a few females on that seven-day adventure, she would standout among the rest.

To repeat myself, I was on a city tour, it was 7:05 PM, and she had already been on the bus when I arrived, so I sat in the seat in front of her. She quickly gave me a smile, standing up, and asked if she could sit with me. She was as petite and cute as a sparrow.

Soft spoken, slow and witty with chosen words, if not editing herself; her introduction seemed most sensitive, and curious. The bus had to go to several hotels and pick up other people for the city tour, and in so doing, she seemed to do most of the talking, if not asking many questions.

I told her about my hometown, and state, being: St. Paul, Minnesota, and my high school, along with how cold it was back there in Minnesota, implying it was like living in the Arctic, which is not far from the truth;—and how my life had turned when I left San Francisco, and got drafted, and now was stationed in an Ordnance Company in Vietnam.

She explained she was from a small farm outside of Sydney; and, that seemed to consume most of our bus time during the first thirty-minutes of our getting to know one another. Actually we were finding out we were both very easy to talk to, which she seemed quite taken by.

We were now sitting, or so it seemed, a little closer together than we were in the beginning, looking out the window as the woman guide pointed out a few things.

Her hair was silky blond, very slim, and a creamy light completion. Her lips were thick and very sexy looking.

I told myself, as I was thinking, remembering what I had said to Rosalie, the Guide, which was, "...what's the use in going on a tour with young girls, when you only got a week in the city. What can you do?" She simply laughed and said, "Have fun, that's what you're here for." But I was now glad I let her persuade me to go, I was having fun. And I liked Zolinda.

As we continued on the tour I maintained my posture, and was kind of show-ing off my brown leather jacket, with long fringes like Wild Bill Cody, and his Wild West Show–I saw on T.V. I had it especially made for this occasion, or may I say, vacation, plus I'd take it home with me when I left Vietnam, and back home it would cost three times as much as what I had paid for it. I figured it was a good investment. It was tailed made in South Korea for me—, I suppose I showed off to her a little too much, being proud of it, but it was really the only nice thing I had in the world. If she had noticed my little arrogance, she never showed she did, or complained about it.

By and large, I think I was not used to being with round-eyed girls and one that was well mannered. I felt like I was more the barbarian, therefore I played a little hard to get, but not too hard. Plus, I was not going to try and get laid, she was in high school, and I was in my early twenties.

I commented [soothingly], "You are really fresh looking, stunning...."

She said with surprise and delight, and a little laughter [contentedly], "I've never heard anyone say that before, I think that's good, right?" I nodded my head with a smiling-grin, implying yes it was good.

[Puzzled] "How come you came on such a tour?" I asked her.

[Aghast—but attentively] She said with a little disappointment in her face,

"Well, to be honest, this is my first tour, and I had heard many of my senior classmate High School [girls] talking about it, and how polite American GI's are, and I asked my grandmother, who is ill now, and my father and mother—we all live together you know; anyway, I asked them if I could, and they agreed I could, at least one time. And so here I am. I just wanted to have some fun. And I'm having it now."

The night was not over yet, but I wanted to make a little move so I asked, "I'd like to see you tomorrow, if that's all right with you and your parents."

She smiled saying, "I'd like that very much," and I'm not sure who took whose hand, but we ended up holding hands on the bus now.

The Bar—The Hippie

As we all sat in the bar, the tour folk that is, the girls having coke and other soft drinks, and I with a cold beer, I left the group for a moment to go to the bathroom. As I came back out, having combed my hair, five men came up to me, asked where I was from, I said the states, "...why?" they seemed to circle me after asking that question.

[Appalled, with a scornful voice] "We don't like hippie's here that's why!" Said one of the brave; I started to walk away, but they quickly surrounded me, and then I figured here we go. I've always been a fighter, sort of a fighter that is, but this was turning out to be a no win battle.

[Talking nervously, yet stern] "You all want to fight one man, how about one at a time or you're only tough with a group backing you up;—I fought bigger guys than you in Vietnam, who's first?"

[Laconically] "Wha'dya-sa...," said one of the men half drunk, trying to find his self confidence.

[Boldly now, with a rush of a fighting spirit] "I said I fought better men than you in Vietnam, who's first?"

"You're a soldier from Vietnam," another asked.

"Yes, why?" I was now encircled [this was curtains I told myself], and they were too tight against me to do much kicking or punching, there was no real way to fight my way out of this circle of bodies, I would have a hard time moving anything, what I could do is jump down, I mean, stoop low, hit a few groins, knock them balls to Mars, and take a beating, that was the best I expected to do now.

As the men started to look at me, it dawned on them, they had troops over in Vietnam, and so what was their '*beef*' over me...[I had the hippie look, the long hair].

"Let's see you're ID, said a man,"

And I pulled it out,

[Looking towards the other men] "Damn Joe, he is, man o man, I'm sure sorry soldier, I mean real sorry, let's buy this man a drink on us." And then all of a sudden they were all buying me drinks, patting me on the back, and had every-thing good to say about me. I shook my head, thinking, what a life, from the fry-ing pan to the snack bar.

Zolinda was looking over by me I had noticed. I think she was scared for me but didn't know what to do, and now confused about everyone being friendly. As I said my goodbyes to them, telling them I had to join the group, Zolinda, asked [with a voice that seemed to be coming out of a light panic state],

"I thought you were in trouble for a moment!" And she grabbed my hand, and pulled me to the group, "Why not stick with us," she added. [It did seem safer.]

The Party's Over

The tour and the party was over, the tour guide told the group whoever wanted to stay there at the bar, they could, except the high school kids, and so I left with Zolinda. We talked again on the way back to the hotel, and she assured me we would see each other around 4:00 PM tomorrow, after school. But it wouldn't work out that way. Her grandmother was ill, and the tour guide got a hold of me and told me she was under obligation to remain home and care for her grandmother. I found out her number and called her and just reassured her I had a good time. She didn't ask me for my address, and I didn't offer it. It was a one time meeting, but for some reason she had taken a little of me with her I think, as I most assuredly took a little of her. I guess if things in life do not work out, it is good if one can take the best out of a person, for we often have a long journey ahead, we might be able to use it.

Maybe her parents didn't want her to get involved with me, she was like a rose ready to blossom, and her hard looking breasts were almost fully developed, along with many other womanly features. She was a prize in a confused world, and I respected her for staying home with her grandmother, if that was truly the case, and if it wasn't, I still had a grand time.

14

The Park in Queensland

[Sydney]

Several boats were along the sides of the lagoon—-or so it looked kind of like a lagoon, but then maybe it was more of an inlet,—none the less, several small boats were tide nice and neat to the dock area, along with several boats out in the lake type atmosphere of the water. The sky was—was romantically rich with clouds hanging over like white umbrellas, and shades of blue like mirrors reflecting back and forth, one matching the other from the waters to the sky, made for a lit up day:—everything reflected blue [my color].

A huge tree decorated the main area of the park; it was like if Rip-Van-Winkle had been resting there for 20-years,——it was all so serene;—The sun making its way between the clouds and the blues and the trees;—the warm wind soaping my face. I pulled out my small Polaroid camera and took several pictures, then noticed a woman near by me, she seemed to be interested in me—, she came walking over towards me, about five foot four inches, slim, brown hair, with glasses, her skirt hugged her legs as the wind pushed between them, and her light scarf was loose around her neck; then stepping within a few feet in front of me, she introduced herself, "Hello," she said softly, an older woman, maybe thirty-five at best,

Then—

Hearing my accent, realizing I was an American [after a pause], she become even more interested in me [dropping her guard], and thinking with my long hair I was in Sydney on some kind of business. Evidently, I was learning I did not look like a GI at all.

When I told her I was an American GI from Vietnam, she seemed to have been let-down a bit [became a little stiffly]. I think she was looking for a Berkley graduate, too bad, she was a fine looker, and I just didn't have the right DNA.

And so I walked around the park, looked at the gulls gliding through the air; moreover, I continued my stroll along the shore line, talking to myself, singing,

69

humming; grabbing the moment, for one must not let themselves down, because the woman will not dance with you. No need to do much else, just go about your business I always say, it was all here, the moment, the camera, the sun the trees the water, it was at best intoxicating; the woman, well, a plus, a conversation. What would I do with her anyway?

15

The New Zealand Maids

I did find out I had the *run* of the hotel, well, for the most part anyway. Two maids, Rena and Hanna, sisters from New Zealand, 18-years old would come into my hotel room in the morning to make my bed, clean my room, and we became good friends quickly. Most of the time I'd either meet them as I was leaving, or they'd actually wake me up, which was good because I didn't want to sleep this R & R away.

They were soft spoken, assured of themselves, and both with wavy long black hair. Hip to the tune, tone and fashion of the day;—fun loving, high energy. The older of the two, which surely was only by a few minutes at best, was hard to tell, for them, although were fraternal twins, yet, with a lot of similarities, was Rena.

Rena seemed to have taken more of a liking to me than her sister, or maybe felt sorry for me, in either case; she liked talking a lot with me. She and her boyfriend, of sorts, took me out to the ocean front one day, there we had a picnic, took pictures, and looked at the mermaid on the rock, looking out into the waves. As always I grabbed the moment, and sat on the huge rock overlooking the ocean, the city was to my left side as Rena snapped a picture.

I didn't want to go back to Vietnam I suppose, but I never thought not to, even though a few folks stopped me here and there, on the side walks streets informing me to stay in Sydney;—I suppose most GI's had to think of returning, and to my understanding, there were many here who had deserted. But that also was not in my DNA; I never thought of that as an option, they did for me. History would not record such a coward's deed by me.

The day would end, and a few more would be left; that is all I thought about, it really never occurred to me to desert.

The girls came back to my hotel room, and we all sat on the roof, drinking from my little refrigerator that they stocked each day with beer, wine and a greater assortment of those little bottles of rum and scotch. From the roof you could see the whole section of this city, within a city, called Queensland, it

71

seemed the small harbor that looked like a lagoon to me was the most beautiful spot in the world, other than possible Como Park, back home in St. Paul, Minnesota. I was not yet twenty-four, but it was right around the corner, and somehow I felt much older, much worldlier, traveled if you will.

16

The Bar-Party and Demi

I met Demi and her friend at the local pub [bar], I was sitting alone and she had asked me to dance; actually I was observing all along one blond [staring at her]. She was who was trying to put the make on a young man, a blond also, both around nineteen years old. I had drunk the night away for the most part. And when the man paid her no attention, she got frustrated, and had asked me to dance, to make him jealous, she had told me so. In any case, she was much more attractive than Demi, but Demi was paying me more attention [and this girl was in a gloomy bellyache over a stranger], and respect than the other woman. And the blond had come right out and said she was going to make it with that man, one way or another. And I wasn't the one to test fate.

Funny I thought, when a woman has her eye on you, in most cases she will walk through the gates of hell to meet her objective. And so I knew I had no way of winning anyway, plus I didn't have time for games or time to win her over. Another philosophy I had picked up somewhere along life's presently short-little-road, was: 'Don't compete if you can't,' it's simply wasted energy. And so it was a good show, that being, watching her sway her hips and cat eyes along his shadow, wherever he went. He knew she was following, and was teasing her I think.

Actually this was the second bar they met at, and he was thinking about going to another, and one of her girlfriends said she over heard what bar he was going to. And that was the one she was going to.

Demi was about 5'3" inches tall, not heavy, but I'd say about 10-pounds over what I'd have liked her to weigh, and she was always laughing, talking, as friendly as a church mouse. The blond gal who was after the blond guy, had big breasts, and a wonderful ass, was far from friendly, although she was, and then she wasn't:—let me explain,—she was not what she was pretending to be, rather she was editing her every move to be what the blond guy wanted. [With an unhappy pause.] She focused then back on the blond-guy. She didn't have much fun I would think;—a challenge yes, but fun, no [but then we all have our own way of having fun]. Now on the other side of the coin, she was friendly, that is to say, as long as you allowed her to be in charge. In consequence, I got the better deal for the time allowed I figured.

Demi and I caught a taxi over to my hotel room. [She was kissing me in the back seat.] When we got there, she undressed, she looked even better than I thought. Yet she was plane looking for the most part, with a fairly better body than I expected [lying desperately and convincingly she wanted me], nice round and full breast, healthy looking. We made love for hours on end, until we both passed out. She snuck a few times over to my little frig-where I had the little bottles of rum, whiskey, and wine, some vodka, and gin. From what I gathered she'd prefer hard liquor to beer, my choice was not the hard liquor or as I call them the devilish chemicals. Demi was closer to my age, or a bit younger, but not much younger, possible twenty-one.

The next day we got up, went out and had breakfast;—in the process I kind of dodged the twin sisters from New Zealand, not wanting to 'show and tell.'

Demi brought me down to the dock area of Sydney, an area I hadn't seen yet. We ate at a few restaurants and again had a few beers, it was a full day.

That evening both Demi and I went to a house party [within the city of Sidney]. When we got there she introduced me to several of her friends [as she hurriedly pronounced their names, of which I'd surely forget by morning], I had my cool leather jacket on, I bought for this R & R, it was sharp and I got a lot of comments on it while being in Sydney.

As the night went on I found myself getting drunker than I expected. There were several rooms in the house, and I seemed to be in this one main room, seemingly bigger than the others, and it seemed to me this was where all the talking was going on.

The Big Room

The following morning [looking at my watch], it was 9:00 A.M;——I shook my head [pried my eyes open], I was lying down next to a radiator-heater I could feel the head on my face; I had passed out but a few inches from it, the following evening. My left hand seemed hot also, as I pulled myself out of my curled up fetus-type position. I quickly moved my hand then. As I turned my head to look at my hand and what happened, I noticed my leather jacket had a huge black spot on it,—as I looked closer—trying to open my eyes up wider, they seemed to be a bit glued to my skin, my blinking was in slow motion—I tried to focus on where the hot burning was coming from, and noticed a burnt black spot on my fore-arm. I quickly pulled my hand to my face from off the heated radiator, of which it was leaning against…staring at it [dissatisfied].

"Shit…it's ruined!" I said out loud [yet no one was there to hear me anyways]; then looked around the big room. It was vacant, I was alone, even Demi had deserted me;—or should I say, left for a better time else where I imagine. On one hand, as I looked back at my left arm and the jacket, I guess I felt lucky; if I was that drunk, I could have burnt myself quite bad, for the heat was penetrating all the way through the leather, and the shirt I had on, had I not had the jacket on, and being so drunk, I may not have even felt my flesh burning.

Wouldn't that be a joke to my friends back in Cam Ranh Bay, I survive through the Vietnam War only to get hurt on R & R. No way, I'd never live it down. I knew of a few people who had shot their toes off, and broke their hands so they could go back home, but it just wasn't in my code, you know, that DNA thing, or values, something like that.

The Jacket

[Anxiously, looking at my jacket again-out of my mouth came] "Shit, shit, shit," [a pause] "…my poor jacket":—specially made in Korea for me, for this trip. I can't believe it. The more I gained my senses and focus, the more I was get-ting madder at spoiling my jacket;—I had paid over $100-dollars for it.

It had gold colored loops for fastening it across the chest area, which hooked to the other side; it had those long dangling fringes like the cowboys such as "Buffalo Bill Cody;" and I mean long, maybe several inches. But now it was ruined

for the most part. I tried to tuck it away for a moment, I felt it was a blast of a night, and got back up on my feet, and found my way slowly to the doorway. Outside I walked a ways down the sidewalk, and caught a taxi to my hotel; the taxi woman told me how the women in Sydney liked Americans because they appreciated them more than their own men. When I got to hotel, I bid her fare-well, and went to my room, whereupon, I discovered I had a few messages from Demi, but I really didn't care, I laid down in bed, took a long nap.

The phone rang about 2:00 PM, it was Demi again, and she wanted to meet me; she implied she'd be down in an hour and we'd make love again. I used the excuse she abandoned me, so I didn't feel guilty about getting rid of her, and told her point blank I needed to be left alone. She was nice, but I just didn't want to hang with her forever. I had about 36-hours left on my seven day R & R and I just wanted to drink it up.

Colleen

Right after I hung up from Demi, Colleen, a friend of Demi called and asked if I'd take her to a certain night club. I really couldn't remember who she was, or what she looked like, but I said "ok," and told her to meet me at my hotel, since I would get lost trying to find any other place.

And so she showed up at 6:00 PM. She was not at all what I had expected. Demi was fair, but Colleen was next to homely.

'Now what do I do,' I told myself;—I had about 33-hours left, and so I told myself to make the best of it

she sat on my bed as I put my shirt on,—she was slender I had noticed, and had breasts the size of a nice rounded coffee-cup. She stood about 5' 4"; an older woman of about 28-years old. She explained [she had talked to me last night after Demi had left] I had given her my phone number, and that was how she got it.

No sooner had I put my shirt on, she was taking off her blouse, and pants. Everything was black, her blouse, her bra, and her panties. She then lay on the bed and asked me to join her. I was a bit horny I think, matter-of-fact, I was as horny as a dog with two dicks, I almost tripped getting to the bed, and climbed between her legs faster than Santa comes down a chimney.

"Calm down," she said, "You're an animal." She was right I was an animal for that split moment, and so I confirmed with her I was, and being so, wasn't sure why I was; and then she said with her teeth mashing, "I'm ok with it, [she paused] just don't rip me," she ended.

We had sex, and it was hard sex for some reason, and afterwards she was hurting a little, and I apologized, not quite knowing what had over taken me. It was not like I hadn't had sex in the last few days, for I had. But instead of trying to figure it out, I dropped it in file #13 [the waste basket], and smiled.

✱

That night we went to a fine night club, she had picked it out, I think because she wanted the best of the best, while she could get it, and I went along with it. And again I got drunker than a skunk; we had two pictures taken, and asked the photographer to send me my picture via Vietnam. Then after the club we went back to my hotel room and screwed again. This time I was a little more graceful, and tender, but probably not much more, for I had passed out. In the morning, I said my farewells, and had to get ready for a 2:00 PM flight back to Vietnam.

17

The Bill

A week in the city was like going from a winter storm to a summer resort; it was appreciated, I even silently thanked the tax payers [mentally] back in America for the free trip. I never claimed I deserved it, but I took it none the less.

I didn't really have much rest either, feeling I'd get enough if, or rather when I got out of the Army, which was not all that far away.

The hotel and its owner were very kind. The New Zealand girls were kind and the farm gal was kind. Demi was gracious for the most part and I had drunk more than my share. Matter of fact, I noticed my bill was $35.00. I didn't have any way to pay the bill, and so when they told me [the owner], about the bill, I think I must have made a few faces. Thirty-five dollars was not a lot of money to a lot of people, but it wasn't a drop in the bucket either, especially for a Corporal in the Army. I was making about $345 tax free a month, but most of it I put in the company safe.

Well, the owner didn't seem to mind, a young black-haired gentleman, of about 35-years

he said, with a smile, and assurance he would get the money,

"No problem soldier, I'll have you sign this note, and we'll forward it to your company, and they will take it out of your pay check." That seemed easy I thought.

I smiled at him, as he gave me the note to sign. He then helped me with my luggage, which was only one bag, and took me to the airport,—walked me into the waiting area, we then shook hands and he was gone to another section waiting for an arriving plane, like he did the first day I came into Sydney.

The weather was warm, and it seemed like it all happened too quick to be true, but I had a few pictures to prove it did happen, not many, maybe a dozen or so, but that was enough [and I loved the brown leather shoes my black sergeant friend borrowed me to go on this R&R with, I would thank him when I got back—they were very expensive.];—here I was leaving, and I felt I had just arrived. I think time slows down when you're actively on a vacation of sorts, that is—in motion on such a trip, and when you stop to look at it, time catches back up with you.

The Army took care of its own that was a slogan and it was a good one, and a true one. And for the most part, I would always have good feelings about Sydney and its people. I figured someday I'd look back at this trip, maybe never come back, but look back, look at the pictures. The two gals I met, the twins, took me to the ocean front, would stay in my memory banks, or at least one of them would; the park and it's big tree, with the woman that was looking for a soul mate. Who knows, a soldiers life is not easy, but then it has its rewards, and traveling was a good perk I thought. If only I could now capitalize on the free education they offered, but that would be looked at another day, when I got out of the Army I suppose. Actually I didn't know it at the time, but it would be used to its extreme.

"Flight 601!"
That's my flight I told myself. They called it again; got to go.

18

Saigon-Going Home
The Cage and the Stranger

[Vietnam]

Just when I thought everything was back to normal, in the process of leaving Vietnam, sitting in the packed-air terminal, going through three days of the military checking of this and that to see if I had any issues in the area of drugs, psychological or physical; consequently, putting me in one cage after another, separating me from one group to another, finally I made it, that is, I made it to the inside terminal, a feat in itself,—I mean...I was really warn out.

During the processing, one guy [GI] came up to me in the bathroom where we all had to piss in this container and give it to the Security Police at the entrance, upon one's departure from the latrine, then they'd have it checked for drugs. If you had any kind of dope in your system, [god forbid] it would come out showing, and you'd have a long wait before you got that free steak in your out-processing at Fort Lewis

a man next to me a young [anxious] white lad, asked me to save some of my piss for him, that is, put it in his container, as he was holding it in his hand [impatiently]. I looked to my right, the guard was always looking everywhere, he'd start on one side go down to the floor with his eyes and up to the ceiling, or almost that high, across and up the other side, and continue doing that; then look outside a bit, and do it again. At the same time, as the guard was doing this, he'd grab the piss bottles of soldiers leaving the bathroom, and give them to another Security Police person and he'd take them away.

For the most part, there was only a few seconds to make such a transfer, if one was going to do it in the first place; that is, making any transfers of the liquid from one bottle to another. The Security Policeman, standing at the doorway, had firmly said, when each person came through,

"...if you are caught giving away you piss, you will be put in jail, along with the fellow you're trying to help..." and we'd not leave this hell hole. I told the guy standing next to me, in a somewhat, panic, to move on, get away from me or I'd exploit him for what he was trying to do, I said this as the guard started to look my way.

"What's going on over there?" The guard said [craftily], as he started to walk towards us. The man next to me [desperately] seeing the movements of the guard, put his hand under the other guy's dick to catch his piss, and quickly maneuvered on over to the other side of the latrine, where there were parallel urinals. [I think the guard overhead me telling him to get away from me quick or else.]

"Something wrong Corporal?" asked the guard. I looked at the dope addict, slyly, and said no, just attending to my own business. "Good," he commented, "Then move on out of here."

The other man now was on the other side of the bathroom, trying to fill the rest of the bottle up in the urinals, he needed to fill it up a little over the middle line, but now the guard was suspicious. When I left, I turned around to catch a glance; the guard was watching him directly. I shook my head as I walked past the gate to get into another processing area; I'm sure the guard knew the man was up to no good, but it was best to just move on.

For three days [at times somewhat bored] I went through this process of check, and recheck. I couldn't even find any booze to drink.

Then on the third day I was put into a cage with three other GI's as there were several of them. They were [the cages] as big as a small kitchen, possible 100-square feet. As they [the processing people] got to you, you would go to another cage, until you got through the whole gamut, three cages in all [to insure you were drug free, this process was started in the summer of 1971, just prior to my leaving which was in the fall].

The Stranger

[Abruptly.] "Hello, my name is Star." I looked at the stranger, he sat to my left, and actually I only turned my head slightly to get a glimpse, giving him a preferred profile incase I didn't want to talk. As I looked at this stranger wide-eyed now, he seemed calming; at the same time, I was listening to the sounds of the airplanes, their engines, and the chatter from within the terminal, the sounds of walking feet, pacing feet,—pacing back and forth, just waiting to get on the flight, everyone was doing it but me, and here was this small man 'Star', youthful, inquisitive. I thought at the moment, now what does he want. Maybe he was twenty-one, maybe not. I was twenty-four now, had been for a week. He looked like he was built solid. He was in green-fatigue Army garb. Not dressy at all but kept, no rank, no anything signifying who he was. I wasn't much for talking, but I guess I could be friendly I thought.

"Hi," I countered back, with a smile, hell I thought I'm on my way home; if he wants to rob me I could care less. I say that facetiously, for I knew it was not his intention. He was most likely boarded like me, having to go through all this gobbledygook bull shit.

He smiled [wisely], his face was smooth, almost illuminated it seemed, so clean looking, too clean looking, I figured he was not an ordinary soldier, maybe one of those undercover Military Intelligence chaps, but so what if he was—I thought.

He said [soothingly],

"I say—it's over for you I see; the war that is, you're going home I expect?" Knowing that was more of a statement than a question, I nodded my head 'yes', and smiled. At best, it was a rhetorical question, in the sense:—it was not a matter of if, rather of when, which was happening at this very moment. I got a little more composed, and asked [a little carelessly],

"How about you, I mean are you, are you headed on home also?"

"I'll be back here, one way or another, I'm sure—it all depends…('Flight…' some one said quietly.) Do you believe in God?"

I thought, man oh man, a preacher in the middle of the airport, maybe one of them you find back home; I've seen them all dressed up in old looking garb, like in the days of Jesus, sandals and all preaching around the airport, going into fast-food restaurants and asking for hand outs. But he couldn't be one of them, he didn't fit the bill.

"Yaw, I guess I kind of know of Him—" adding, "I've said a few prayers in my time." Actually the only time I prayed was when I was young, and was studying to be an altar-boy, and when I drove drunk, and a few times here in Vietnam. But I felt I need not explain all that.

He smiled again, as if he knew something I didn't know, or knew something I knew and wasn't willing to share, he wasn't snobby, or impolite, and I seemed to be in a trance as he continued to talk, and everything seemed to be related to a solitude with God. What could I say I told myself, I had nothing better to do today, and I wasn't sure what they were saying over the loud speakers but it wasn't let's go, it's 9:00 AM, but it was getting close to my time to get on the plane I knew. His voice was comforting, and tranquil.

Forty-five minutes later

[Bewildered.] "Excuse me," I said to the stranger, as I got up and went to the counter asking why I wasn't being called to get on the 9:00 AM flight, it was now 8:55 AM. She looked at me strangely [almost amused], then scratched her neck, saying [as she tried to clear her throat]:

"Everyone is aboard the airplane, we made last call 15-minutes ago;—it looks like you'll have to take the next flight out, sorry."

[Un-thoughtfully I yelled.] "What!" A few of the soldiers around the counter looked my way. "What's that?" I asked in disbelief. Then settling...slowly calming myself down...I continued to speak:

"I mean lady that was my flight; I need to get on it [I didn't stop to focus, and listen to what she had said]."

"Sorry soldier, it's all secure, and ready to take off, you really can not get on it."

I took in a deep breath of air, and let it out slowly.

"Oh well," I said, trying to be cheerful, and then walked away. That's what I get for talking, I told myself. The next flight was at 9:00 PM, I had time to walk around and get a sandwich and some coffee, they had a few carts with Vietnamese women selling food, and some machine venders. But as I looked for my friend in this somewhat 2600 to 3000 square foot waiting area, I couldn't see him. No way could he have left, unless he decided to stay in Saigon, at this air base [Tan-son-nut].

Sitting Thinking Waiting for the Flight

I sat back down, got thinking how slow time moves when you're patiently waiting; telling myself, this time will all pass, and be but a memory in time to come, you know, this was simply how it was [plaintively but true].

My mind now was shifting to a few days ago, I had met a gal with a blue dress on a few days ago, she wanted me to go down to her house in the city of Saigon, it would be a lustful afternoon at best, and if caught, a bust at worse, that is to say, I could get in trouble. Not sure what her price was, she said we'd argue about it later, she was a doll, big round breasts poking out of her flimsy silk like dress, a little like Frenchie, with nice sculptured legs. She came into the men's latrine right behind me, she was a secretary to some Command Sergeant Major I believe, she kept on telling me we could do it right in one of the stalls there, right in the huge Air Force, latrine [actually who would know or tell, many women came in and left, all supposedly working—but I said no, it was too wild for me, but really meaning, too careless.]

Joe, my friend from the 611th followed me here to the Air Base, and was going to Hawaii, where he was going to meet his wife. He told everyone back at base camp, he was done with the Army, saying,

"Chick, don't tell anyone. Make sure you don't tell anyone, they gave me $2500 to stay in, and I took it."

He seemed to be in a little panic as he emphasized not telling anyone, he even told me to 'shut up' about it a few more times, almost sorry he told me in the first place—that I was the only one he was telling [he was regretting—and here I'm telling everyone in the book, 33-years later]. I told him it was great, if that's what he wanted; not sure what the big fuss was about, but I'm sure he cut the Army down from head to toe, and you know, that made it worse when you turn around a join right back up. In any case, he made sergeant, we were both corporals at the 611th; I think the extra strip he got was for joining. For myself, I needed to get out, it was time. He had taken a flight yesterday; I figured he was in Hawaii right this very minute.

Flight A102/9:00 PM

As I got ready to get on board the 9:00 PM flight, information had come back, seeping through the ranks, the grapevine as one might say,—it was that the previous flight had gone down in a storm before it reached Japan; sadly but true...

I stood like a stick in disbelief—

[With profound disgust.] I had to be pushed by the soldier behind me to wake up; I think I was in a daze for a moment.

"I was supposed to have been on that flight," the soldier behind me caught his breath, "No kidding." As I would find out later in life, this would happen once more; in 1980, flying back from Italy to Germany, and back to New Jersey. I would take an early flight out of Italy, not the one I would be assigned to because I had gotten to the air base early, and they had several seats available, and asked me if I wanted to take it. I'd find out in Frankfurt, that the plane I was suppose to have been on, after my flight, went down.

In this flight [from Vietnam to Japan I was suppose to have been on], there were 220-soldiers killed;—in the flight from Italy to Germany [to take place in 1980], over 240-soldiers would be killed.

Anyhow, I shook myself sober, and forced myself onto the flight, walking slowly, and thinking about the 220-soldiers, and my friend who had disappeared. I guess life would be boring without mystery, and so I left well enough alone. It was the hand of providence that rearranged things, not sure why, I was no better than another soldier, by far. Matter of fact, I was probably worse than most. But I knew I couldn't dwell on that too long, it was just the way things were.

19

A Steak at Fort Lewis

As I was on the flight, going to Fort Lewis from Vietnam I knew once I'd get to Lewis, I'd process out of the Army, get a de-briefing, and be on my way home. It was the way things worked. If anything I had lots of time to think of the future. I started to think as the plane went over more land and water on its way to Japan [where it would refuel and I would buy my mother a beautiful opal necklace and earrings], and then onto Alaska [to refuel again], I thought about a reoccurring dream I had while in Vietnam. It was about being in the back section of a plane, and somehow the plane had lost its upper section in mid air. The dream never went past that [I had it several times]. Maybe this was the plane I thought, but I was seated in the middle of the plane not the back, it couldn't be the same plane, or dream. Funny what you think when information is constantly being processed in your brain.

Two hundred soldiers dead in a flight, a preacher of sorts talked me into missing a plane. I was about to process out of the Army. The dream may have been right, the plane I was meant to be on went down, and possible I would have been in the back, like my dream indicated. It never had an ending [my dream, as I have already said] because, maybe and just maybe, God tore that part of the page out of the book of life [After I would arrive home from Vietnam, I'd never have that dream again for the rest of my life, or up to this writing, anyway.]

War is never good, but I had really gone to Vietnam thinking it would free a country; what I had learned was peace does not mean freedom, for they had peace, as long as they did what the dictator told them to do, yes, then he gave them peace [meaning North Vietnam of course]. At best I felt, maybe a slice of Democracy with a slice of Capitalism could benefit Vietnam. I didn't know the combination for them, what would work, and I'm not sure if anyone else did either.

But what I did know was such regimes did not give the people, [although in pretense they may have] peace with freedom, something they never knew in the first place, but it seemed to me like they wanted to test it out; possible something new for that whole part of the world in general. Why the world was willing to let a dictator hold this country in ransom was beyond me;—especially when the nations doing the squabbling were the countries that had peace with freedom. It was a time of countries domineering people, and in some cases countries dominated countries. Who was right and who was wrong would be talked about for many years to come. Wiping my brow, I sat back and enjoyed the sun coming through the window.

Maybe the whole world couldn't tell the difference between peace for sale, and peace with freedom [sometimes we're just too close to the forest to see the trees].

In my short life time, I have witnessed at points of time, where the whole world was wrong and one person right, it has been proven time and again. But I didn't know if I was right or wrong, I just went by my values, I couldn't violate them. And so maybe our truth is simply our values that are what makes us right and wrong. I don't know, in any case I was glad to be going home.

I looked at a few clouds outside of my port hole in the plane; it looked like a cluster of candy frost. I liked it. Still no birds though. [I hesitantly looked at a number of faces in the seats, some sleeping, some tired, some couldn't sleep, but all happy to be getting out of Vietnam, I think.]

My mind started shifting into day-dream mode again.

I think all my friends in Vietnam would not have cared dying for that reason alone, that is, peace with freedom. I knew all the controversy back home was more on blind-sight, and hind sight. A bunch of people blind following the blind not free thinking. The very same way the government runs the war, the blind leading the blind.

From what I've seen, read, and heard most of it was showmanship, news on news, the spot light. We all forgot people were dying. We forgot peace with freedom. We all had our sins though.

The sorry feeling I always carried around was [although it didn't bother me as much as my friends] was the naked fact we had no support, not by our own people, much less the rest of the world.

I got thinking about the steak you are supposed to get the last day in the Army, no, I mean, when you come home from Vietnam, I guess everyone gets one. I hope they are right.

I had also learned,—and thought as I sat on this stuffy plane, with all the body odor shifting around like in a horse stall, and believe me, it was enough to kill a skunk—no one knows you as a soldier;—that is to say, because while working in San Francisco, at Lilli Ann, everyone in the world knew of, or about Adolph Shuman even me, I worked for him, but here in the Army I was no more known than a 'wino' on Wabasha Street, in St. Paul, Minnesota. And I'm sure if Mr. Shuman would have been on this airplane with me, no one other than a few people on the plane would have known him. So that told me something for having a long career in the Army. But I knew I needed to get educated somehow and I would take advantage of the GI Bill now and go to College. That is what I had to do.

The world was changing and you had to change with it. To have a degree, and not be licensed in some profession, you were not in demand. Plus, I needed to learn how to be more assertive, and talk to crowds, and so I had a lot of work ahead of me.

◊

When I got to Fort Lewis, I was given a big fat steak [and I don't mean with a lot of fat on it], just like they promised, and some letters from the President saying what a good job I did, and from a few Generals and so on. I was also told they'd send me an Army Accommodation Medal in the mail in a few months, and then I was on my way to St. Paul, Minnesota, it took all of 24-hours.

20

Back Where I Started

[Last words-St. Paul, Minnesota]

§

When I got off the plane in St. Paul, Minnesota, and crossed the road to get into the cab to take me home, I almost got hit by a car. A driver of another car stopped, saw me in uniform and said [caringly]:

"Be careful soldier, we had a Vietnam Vet cross the street yesterday, and got killed."

I've always been on one hand careful, on the other carelessly cautious, but normally I've never been sort of—sort of in a daze; but I seemed to be now. Funny how things work out, you go through the training, a war, only to come home and get killed by a driver the day you get back. In any case, I went home, it was as I liked it, expected it to be, I remember the very thoughts that were going through my mind that first day home, when I got out of the cab, just staring about: it was as though dawn had come among the city,—for the birds were singing—.

I looked in my backyard and within the vicinity, [trying to grab the moment—still in that daze] and yes, there they were, perched on the lilac bushes chirping, tweeting, peeping [interrupting one another], on the telephone wires, on the roof on the garage, the house, it seemed I could spot them all over the place, and they all were singing, singing, singing [as if they had just noticed me]. Funny, I had lived here all my life and never heard them sing like this before.

✳

It was the second evening at my mother's house;—I sat on the porch thinking, listening to the birds sing, staring out the screened-in-windows. Grandpa was pacing the floor, he had been in WWI, my uncle a POW in WWII, and my

89

Uncle Frank was killed in Italy in WWII. And so the whole family knew I suppose about the birds, that they don't sing in combat zones, they never do, not in any wars. Why should they [?]…there is nothing to sing about. But I was lucky; it wasn't bad for me, not like for many others I knew.

Before I left St. Paul to go to San Francisco, in which I went from there into the Army, the neighborhood was my world. It was all I knew of/or about. Now there was a much bigger world out there. I was becoming calm again, as I smoked my cigarette slowly; grandpa pacing in his living room behind me, like he always did. Like he did before I left him.

I told the birds, I was a good soldier, they seem to listen to me, and I told the birds, I liked their singing; plus, they were the only ones that didn't spit at me.

*

YE LITTLE BIRDS

[Back from War]

Here, then, I came back
So they appeared before me;—
But I am no child anymore
'Oh, but I am happy

I see you fly perched
On trees so high—,
As if you know God,
Himself—
Thank you for the blessings…
Ye Little Birds

Here, then, I came back,
[Ye little birds]
To watch you in your blues
Your skies, your waters,
And in trees so high:

I find myself somehow
Entwined with thy;—
With sounds of wings,—
Fading sounds of song:

Caw-caw
Coo-coo
Cluck-cluck

"You are home," they cry.

Tossed images inside my soul,
Floating, floating, no more:
Left behind images of war;—
For the birds do not like wars
[They have told me so]
"Do not depart," they say—
But yet we go,
Time, and time again…

Here, then, I came back to you
Who have never left my mind?

Ye little birds—.

✳

Last Words

Now I must bring you up to date [with Chick Evens], today being May, 2003; and as in everything in life, we must move on. Yes, on, and on we must go, and not think of what might have been, or could have been in Vietnam, if this or if that would have taken place. Without a shadow of a doubt, it could have been handled better by all involved. With all the probabilities that were looked at in the past, during what is now called the Vietnam Era, simply put, a lot of unknown's were looked at. But you got a picture of how I felt at that time, a time I lived through, and the way others felt that were around me, well, by-and-by, as indicated, a hat full of rain. Having said that let me make peace in the following paragraph:

The war started with John F. Kennedy, yes our hero, he planted the first 16,000 American troops into harms way, and Johnson added 8,000 more, in 1965. And from there it escalated to over 500,000. It was what one may have called a little brushfire, turned into a horrific forest-fire [and I doubt Kennedy or Johnson were evil doers, wanting to kill 2,058,000 people, most likely misinformed at best]. Second, let's make peace with Jane Fonda, and all the movie stars that have caused us trouble, in our lives [they, like us soldiers need peace, and surely somewhere in their hearts and minds meant well, or so I'd like to believe; but may the Lord be with them, as well as with us]. And with North Vietnam whom lost 2-million lives compared to our 58,000 American lives. Yes, they paid dearly, and you see, nobody wins. And to Russia and China who had their secret treaties with the North Vietnamese, we surely put them on edge, if not at times in a tight spot, maybe more than a few times. There could have been a WWIII.

Now that I did my apologizing, let's see where we or I am at. Not sure if we have or have not admitted, but if not, it is clear by now, or should be, the war was to produce a "Stalemate [a log jam if you will]" to/with the enemy, in essence, to contain them,—and possible push, or dislodge them; or put another way, to kill them faster then they could re-supply new bodies to fight, thus forcing them to a draw, like in North Korea. It is not a way to fight a war though, so we have learned the hard way. But I think we have learned, and that is the good part; or at least it seems so by the empirical data from the crushing blows we gave in the last three wars, that being, in the Persian Gulf I and II wars, and Afghanistan; with the much more clearer objectives. I am not for war, but if were going to fight one, let's do it right.

No we can not guess, and go to war by inches, or with limits, not anymore. It, not only gives the wrong messages to everybody, to include the ones we call the 'good guys' but to the world as a whole;—it defeats the purpose of all the training of the soldier. You have trained him or her with your tax money,—trained professional, licensed killers. That is what you get for your money, like it or not. A soldier is not paid to play chess; he's paid to be a soldier, 24-hours a day. That is right, if he thinks different, he is in the wrong trade [as some have indicated in the last Gulf war, 2003]. Most of the rest of the world knows this, except the west for some odd reason.

And as we all know, the President we dishonor the most, Nixon [or so it has seemed to me in my 55-years on this earth], is the one that got us out of Vietnam, with what little dignity he could. And to him, possible he deserves a Commendation Medal for Meritorious Service. And so, let dead dogs lay, this has been my story.

End to the Story

"Where the Birds don't sing"

≈

Note: On 4/5/03, on the "Barnes & Noble Top 100" list .com, Mr. Siluk's book: "Romancing San Francisco," was number #66, of more than one-million books.

❋   ❋   ❋

About the Author's Books

Tales of the Tiamat: This is a trilogy, consisting of "*The Tiamat, Mother of Demon*," the second book, "*Gwyllion, Daughter of the Tiamat*," and the third, "*Revenge of the Tiamat*". All three are full of adventures and travels by Sinned, the main character of the three novels, as is the Tiamat involved, yet we see many other antagonists along side of her. The series takes you to Malta, Easter Island, ancient England, and Avalon, where the Tor is being built, Asia Minor, where Yort is, Sinned's home, and a half dozen other places. In addition to the main story of each of these three books, which is being put into one, in the "Tales of the Tiamat," a fourth books was added, called "The Tiamat and the King."

The Chick Evens Sketches: In this trilogy, we have sketches of life that incorporate the late 60's to the early 70's; the hippie generation, the new era, the awakening of Aquarius, the peace era, it has been called many things. In his first book, his sketches, take you on a romance of a city and era, the book being called: "*Romancing San Francisco*" [1968-69], he introduces us to karate's famous Yamaguchi family, to include Gosei, and his father Gogen "The Cat"; along with the famous Adolph Shuman, the once owner of the line of Lilli Ann cloths, along with other sketches. In the other two books, "*A Romance in Augsburg*," and "*Where the Birds don't Sing*," the sketches start where the first book left off, from 1969 to 1970 and to Vietnam in 1971. Here you go to Europe for a Romance with a Jewish German girl, and on to Vietnam where there is a war going on. Mr. Evens will also end up in Sydney, for one week of some great adventures, what the Army called back then R&R. Mr. Siluk spent 11-years in the Army, being a Staff Sergeant when he was discharged, and has lived all three books.

Short Story Collection [s]: this is not a trilogy, rather three books, of which two are similar, that being of Suspense, "*Death on Demand*," of which there are seven stories, and "*Death by Desire*" having ten; and the third book, being a mixture of short stories, called "*Everyday's An Adventure*".

Spiritual: The Author has some strong religious and spiritual views. Having studied and done graduate work in theology, and missionary work in the moun-

97

tains of Haiti, and being at an earlier age an Ordained Minister, his two books, "*The Last Trumpet and the Woodbridge Demon*," being his first book in this genre, talks about experiences of the early eighties, where he had visions concerning end time events that are coming to pass right this very moment. In his second book, "*Islam, In Search of Satan's Rib*," he talks about the ongoing subject of terrorism on America, and the world as a whole, but in a different manner; instead of trying to figure out the mind of the Islamic-Arab, he looks at this god, enmeshed with Islam today.

Addiction: As of this writing [May, 2003], Mr. Siluk is still a licensed Counselor in good standing with the State of Minnesota. He has also held international licenses in Drug's and Alcohol, and has worked for hospitals and clinics in dual disorder facilities. In his book, "A Path to Sobriety, the Inside Passage," which is a common sense book on understanding alcoholism and addiction, the book is an ultimate guide to substance abuse, a powerhouse for preventing relapse and curing the disease. Siluk has been working on a follow up book to his sobriety, and addiction book, called "Prevention," which he may or may not release depending on the need for it.

Travels: Mr. Siluk has travel, or has been traveling I should say for 37-years out of his 55 ½ years of his life to this date. He has traveled 25 ½ times around the world. And in most of his books you can see, feel and almost taste this [to be more exact, he has 613,000-air miles, not to include ground miles]. In his book, "Chasing the Sun," he takes you to a variety of places, by showing you some forty-pictures,—giving you an overall view of his story on how he got started. Each picture has its own caption, and is read for 'a would be traveler', or one who would like to reminisce.

The Beast Books: I wasn't sure what to call these three next separated books, so I named them, the "The Beast Books". For in their own way, they all have their own beast. The first book being, "*Mantic ore: Day of the Beasts*," which is the author's favorite of the three, you step into the demonic underworld. A lot of him is in this book it seems. A touch of Vietnam, a touch of his home town, St. Paul, Minnesota, and invisible shadows that change shapes into animals and human forms. Visions upon visions. In the second book, the "*The Rape of Angelina of Glastonbury, 1199 AD*," you are involved with a suspenseful story of revenge, and at the end of the book is a nice surprise, another story. And for the third beastly book, "*Angelic renegades & Rephaim Giants*," you get just that, no more, no less.

It is a book on the ancient dictators of the world, the ones who have cursed God, to have man worship them.

Out of Print book: For the curious reader; although they are out of print, the author has a few left in storage. "The Other Door," was his first book published, in 1981, a book on poetry. It is a Volume one, of which he is working on volume two, yes, 22-years in the making. This book is so scarce that only 25-copies are left, at a price you most likely not want to pay. Second, is the authors 2nd book, "The Tale of: Willie the Humpback Whale," which got much attention in the 1982 year, although it did not get a Pulitzer Prize, it was an entry, and considered. At present the author is considering a 4th printing, and revised edition. He does have a number of copies available for interested people [a limited number]. And the book "Two Modern Short Stories of Immigrant Life," that is more of a chap book that came out in 1984 as a trial run. Only 100-copies were ever printed, of which one of the stories were printed in the "Little Peoples Press," and then the book was pulled back for personal reasons, and off the market by the author. This very limited book of which there are possible 30-copies left can also be acquired, but again, this overview is more for the inquisitive, than for selling these very rare and hard to fine books.

Visit my web site: http://dennissiluk.tripod.com

You can also order the books directly by/on: www.amazon.com
www.bn.com along with any of your notable book dealers

Front cover art design [drawing] by the author, 1990,—of the view from his hotel in Queens, Sydney, Australia, 1971

0-595-28180-X

Printed in the United States
1512400002B/252

9 780595 281800